THE BRITISH EMPIRE OF
MAGIC

A NOVELLA BY
JOSEPH J. JORDAN

Prologue

Prince Jacob was born to be to the next ruler of the British Empire of Magic but when his mother Queen Ellaryne's crown and country is threatened by foes old and new he finds out that everything he once believed ends up being a lie. He battles his conscience whether to choose his oldest friend or stand by his mothers side.

CHAPTER 1

THE ROYAL COUNCIL OF THE BRITISH EMPIRE OF MAGIC

Twenty years ago...

An emergency meeting of all Royal Council members was called and King Maybook had no choice but to submit. For the first time he would be completely at the mercy of the most powerful people in the Empire and knew he would have to face their judgment for what he had done. The harshest judgement would come from his daughter, the Princess 'Ellaryne Maybook'. Though the King believed his actions were justified to secure his family's dominance over the throne and safety of his people the Royal Council would only judge him for the murder of an entire seemingly innocent family and no one could ever know the truth of why he took their lives.

The Imperial City stands upon a solitary island off the South West coast of England comprising of stunning medieval castles and stone paved streets with the Royal Palace rising imposingly above all else. Invisible to the human eye the Imperial City is protected by ancient magical masking spells casted centuries ago by the most powerful sorcerers in the world to hide their kind from the human world after the Magi Wars ended.

Atop The Royal Palace lies the Higher Palace. Within this towering stone building was the home to the King and his family (the Royal Family) and it was also where the Royal Council convened. Their power and influence was felt throughout the Empire and indeed the world for the British Empire of Magic was the most powerful of Magical Nations in the world.

The King had been accused of murder by none other than the Royal Council themselves. Today his fate would be decided as they met and the future of the Empire would be set.

A huge oval shaped chamber sitting at the very highest point of the Royal Palace is the home of the Royal Council. At its centre a long black stone 'High Table' with twelve empty seats, six either side headed by the thirteenth throne chair for the King. This room had seen over a thousand years of Kings, Queens, their Royal Lords and Ladies pass through making their mark in history to create an Empire of Magic. There has been a Maybook on the throne for over 500 years. Their blood line is of unquestionable and exceptional wielding of magic. It has long been said that the Maybooks are amongst the most powerful sorcerers in history.

The silence of this imposing chamber is broken instantly with the booming of the black stoned doors opening. The royal guards enter the chamber dressed in long dark green robes and smooth silver helmets each holding a golden wielding spear. Eleven royal lords and ladies enter the chamber to take their seats at the 'High Table' closely followed by the Royal Lady Princess Ellaryne Maybook, the King's daughter. A slender figure of grace and strength the Princess took her place closest to the throne seat. Her olive skin and thick long dark hair resting on her shoulders and deep brown eyes focused unwaveringly on her father's seat. Knowing what was to come, the decision she would have to make and what it would cost her.

All the royal lords and ladies were from powerful families possessing regional influence or rare gifted magical talents and in some cases, both. Each earned their place on the Council by nomination from another member or by royal appointment.

Seated opposite the princess was her husband Royal Lord Johnathan. A tall kind faced man desperately trying to catch his wife's gaze, but she was pre-occupied. The murmuring was starting to get louder from the council, whispers of disbelief and outrage began to circulate.

"Silence!"

The Princess demanded and as she rose from her seat her father, the King, had entered the chamber and stood in the doorway flanked by two of the highest ranking officers in the royal guard.

"Proceed, bring the King to his seat and then all guards are to leave us at once," Princess Ellaryne bellowed. She was the highest ranked member of the Council after her father and

heir to the throne. The King a well-set man of average height, a long grey wispy beard and deep dark brown eyes gazing at the stone floor dressed in the finest of dark robes. His hood placed over his head and his golden slender and subtle crown rested in his hands. He motioned towards the throne seat at the head of the High Table and obeying the Princess's command the Royal Guard left, leaving only the Royal Council in the chamber.

"You all know why we have called for the emergency convening of this Council, my father, your King has been accused of the murder of three people. A family no less, the Colsom family. Two adults and a…thirteen year old boy."

Even with her unwavering gaze towards the Council the Princess's voice showed the obvious signs of anger and deep despair.

"The evidence brought forward by the members of this Council is irrefutable of the King's guilt. Given your Royal Position as King I will allow you to speak now of these crimes and how you plead before we proceed with sentencing."

As Ellaryne sat back in her seat the King rose with the command as he ever did but with a great sadness and regret across his face.

"I am guilty." The deep timbering voice echoed through the chamber.

The King and his daughter locked eyes for a second which felt the length of eternity. In that moment her mind was racing with a thousand thoughts of hate and disbelief.

"It has fallen to me as heir and the highest ranking member of this Council to remove you from your Kingship immediately. The law of succession and passing of the crown dictates that I, succeed the King, however, in light of the crimes committed by my father I cannot accept this automatic handover of succession. Instead I ask that this Council to vote for the acceptance or rejection of my ascension to Queen and Empress of this great Empire. The King's sentence will be decided immediately after the vote has been cast."

The Council had not seen a leadership vote in over two centuries. The Royal Lords and Ladies began immediately to stand and voice their votes in the form of yeas and nays. Each taking their turn, the eleven members of council voted.

Royal Lady Kerr, one of the most respected members of the Council was the final to stand and speak. A newly appointed member by Royal Appointment of the Princess's herself. Flashing blue eyes, blonde wavy hair who possessed the power of international influence across the Magical Nations and a long lineage of gifted sorcerers.

"And with my 'Yea' the vote is unanimous. Royal Lady Princess Ellaryne Maybook is to be Queen and Empress of the British Empire of Magic as of now. I call for the sentencing of former King Maybook immediately," softly spoke Royal Lady Kerr.

Now Queen Ellaryne rose from her seat *"Regretfully, my first act as your Queen must be to seek the justice and punishment for my father's crime. Before I do, I think we all deserve an explanation for this, what can only be described as a random act of violence… What say you?"*

His head hanging in shame he softly spoke the words that would haunt the Queen for years to come.

"I did what I had too. The future of our people, our survival was at stake. You cannot understand. I am…I was your King and I bear this responsibility so you do not have too. I accept the ultimate fate."

The Queen knew what he meant by the 'ultimate fate' and it was his way of acting out his last order as King. He was sentencing himself.

"Then the sentence must be death, today, now in this chamber and this responsibility falls to me to act out. But… If the truth of the King's crimes were to become public knowledge, I do not believe this leadership, or indeed our Empire would survive it. It would weaken us in the eyes of the world. Our allies would question the leadership we command for our kind and our enemies would take swift advantage of the chaos and divisions that would inevitably follow. Therefore, the King's crimes and his true cause of death will forever be hidden and you are all to be sworn to Death Vows…This is to protect your people, our Empire…Are we all agreed?"

The Queen took a moment and rested her eyes on each of the members of the Royal Council. All of them silently lowered their heads in approval but some more hesitant than others.

"Then we are decided," said the Queen.

The Queen took a final look at her father, her King. He smiled at her warmly, they both knew this was the only way.

She leaned forward and raised her hand over his heart. The air between her hand and his chest wavered and shifted out of focus. She had began the casting of the spell. She centred herself and allowed the magic to flow from her mind through her body and to pass into her hand and finally into the King. In these final moments she shared with him a memory.

The two overlooking the ocean from the Royal Palace Gardens, staring at the statues of past Kings and Queens that stood hundreds of feet out of the ocean. There were so many they reached over the horizon.

"Each of these men and woman lead their people with their hearts, Ella. They made mistakes as a result of this. This is the way. You'll be Queen soon enough and you'll have to make difficult choices. Draw on the strength and experience of those before you but do not let old beliefs guide you in a new world."

Ellaryne closed her hand tightly, now the space between hand and chest had settled.

The King's heart beats no more. The King was dead.

CHAPTER TWO

QUEEN ELLARYNE'S EMPIRE

Twenty years later...

Prince Jacob critiqued and eyed himself in the mirror, closely examining his appearance. His dark purple robes fell to the floor with fabric to spare. Solid silver armour plating enclosed his neckline and shoulders. His sharp and structured jawline, olive skin, dark eyes and thick dark hair were true genetic traits of his family line. A tall blonde handsome man in his late twenties with bright blue eyes stood behind him smiling and shaking his head. He placed his hand on Jacob's shoulder.

"Yes, Your Highness, you look good!" said Elliot

"Good!? Haha! It's Ascension Day! Twenty years of reign, I better look better than just 'good' for The Queen," said Jacob softly.

"You could go out there with a sack on your head and your mother would still think you look like the 'ONE TRUE PRINCE!!!" Elliot bellowed comically.

Jacob smiled at Elliot through the mirror and turned around to face him. He took Jacob's hand and then pulled him closer to him. Cupping his face firmly in his hands they looked at each other passionately.

"It's because she's proud of you," said Elliot.

They kissed, smiled at each other and hugged. "Come on, let's do this," Eliot motioned towards the door and Jacob followed after letting out a deep breath and placing the thin gold Princes's crown upon his head.

The long sand coloured stone hallway leading to the Royal Palace Gardens was lined with the Royal Guard dressed in their usual green robes and golden Wielding Spears. Floating in the air next to each guard were perfect spheres of fire summoned with magic next to each of the Royal Guards to light the hallway. Jacob and Elliot walked the long hallway together before stopping at the arched entrance the gardens. Jacob could see his mother, the Queen sitting on her throne in the middle of the gardens dressed in white robes, plated with gold armour glistening in the sun. She was surrounded by the Royal Council, leaders from other magical nations and hundreds of other nobles. She raised her hands summoning them to come forward. With her command they walked to her.

"Your Majesty, My Queen. On this your twentieth Ascension Day, I pledge my loyalty and my life to you and the British Empire of Magic." Jacob knelt before his Queen. He raised his head to look at his mother. The Queen closed her eyes and nodded in response. Her face showed only the slightest sign of ageing from the past two decades.

"I accept your pledge to me and this Empire my son," said the Queen.

Jacob rose, he and Elliot joined the rest of the Royal Council at the Queen's side.

"This day marks not just two decades of my reign over this powerful and loving land but over two hundred and twenty years of peace between the Great Nations of Magic. But, perhaps even more important than these achievements is that today we celebrate twenty years since the formation of the first democratically elected parliament by the people of the this British Empire of Magic. Ladies and gentlemen, I present to you the fifty elected members of your Imperial Parliament of Magic."

With this announcement the Queen rose from her throne clapping as the fifty parliamentary men and woman walked into the gardens side by side all wearing matching royal blue robes with the familiar royal crest (the Queen's crown etched around a golden magical orb) on their left arms. They all took their place before the queen and knelt, their heads bowed in respect to the Queen.

Continuing, the Queen said, *"I have heard all of you renew your pledges to me and this Empire today and now I pledge to you all to uphold and continue the peace and equality that our Nations stand for. It is the job of you, the peoples parliament, to hold us, your Royal Council and your Queen accountable and that our actions will always be in the best interests of this Nation of Magic. Do you submit to this responsibility?"*

"We submit, your Majesty!" Parliament responded in perfect unison.

The sounds of cheers and applause erupted from the Royal Gardens as the Queen rose from her throne she looked over her shoulder at the statues of the Kings and Queens before her rising from the ocean. This time a new figure rose from the ocean. Her father's statue stood touching the sky above her.

The Queen walked down from her throne rose her hands in the air she said, *"Now enjoy the festivities my friends. Smile, drink and love!"*

The crowd cheered and waiters appeared with glasses filled with champagne for all. The Queen taking the first glass and raising it to the sky before taking a sip herself.

Jacob walked over to the Queen who was now taking turns in greeting those that had pledged to her. He slowly moved himself in between the sea of pledgers and his mother. At thirty four years of age he had learnt this skill well without seeming to 'get in the way' along with spotting when his mother needed 'rescuing'. She caught his eye and smiled knowingly.

"Ah, my son! if you'd all excuse me I would like a few words with the Prince." The Queen ushered Jacob and herself away from the crowd and strolled along the edge of the gardens overlooking the Imperial City.

"Well? How is the Queen holding up?" Jacob asked.

"The Queen is holding up fine. Your mother on the other hand could do with a whisky and a quiet room!" Answered the Queen chuckling to herself.

"No such luck just yet mother. Just a moments respite with me I'm afraid."

"And that's enough." She linked her arm with his and pulled him closer to her,

"We need to talk about the White Islands," said the Queen.

"You've heard more rumours?" Jacob asked.

"Yes. More than just rumours unfortunately. The Lady Regent Catherine has demanded that we discuss the sovereignty of the White Islands and its separation from the Empire.".

The Queen stopped and looked at Jacob with a look he knew very well.

"Surely you don't expect me to go as your emissary? If you recall, her son-in-law and I are not exactly best friends and I hear he's her advisor now!"

"The fact that you're the reason Neville was removed from the Royal Council is why you are the perfect person to send for these discussions."

"You'll have to explain that one to me," Jacob said confused.

"You will go there under the pretence of hearing out the Lady Regent's 'demands' as she so calls it but undoubtedly your old friend Neville won't resist the chance to throw his new title your way. I want you to take that opportunity to get under his skin a little, which should be easy as you tend to bring out a hate in him. It's been my experience people tend to reveal things in these moments that they wouldn't entertain otherwise. You on the other have a talent of keeping your resolve in these moments. Time to exploit those talents my dear son."

"And what kind of information precisely are you expecting him to unwittingly tell me?"

"The timing of this outburst of independence by the Lady Regent doesn't make sense. There have been vastly better suited moments over the past decade for her to make a move like this, but right now the Empire is strong, united and our allies are committed to us."

"You think she's hiding something?"

"Hiding someone as opposed to something I would expect, an ally of sorts that would strengthen her position would be my guess. Otherwise her pursuing this demand of independence would fail. Ultimately she needs to have the people of the White Islands on her side along with enough Parliamentary support to force the matter. She knows the Royal Council would never agree to a complete separation of our lands, especially the White Islands. As you know, the Islands stand between us and the American threat." The Queen's face couldn't hide the signs of the uneasiness of not knowing what the Lady Regent was hiding.

"Very well, I'll leave in the morning. Oh I do love a reunion!". Jacob said sarcastically, making his mother laugh.

"You never know, he may have forgiven you, now that he is a Lord Advisor!"

"Haha, A Lord... Only because he's married to the Vice-Regent."

The Queen laughed and motioned them back towards the crowd, *"just remember, your father is a Prince only through marriage."*

"Where is he anyway?" Jacob asked.

"Oh you know he hates these things, he's with the spell makers working on something new and life changing most-likely!" replied the Queen.

They chuckled as they parted ways and rejoined the festivities.

Jacob made his way to the edge of the gardens where he found Elliot talking to Royal Lady Kerr.

"Prince Jacob! You're looking good. How are you?" asked Lady Kerr.

"I'm good thank you Camila. You are looking very well as always. What've you two been talking about?"

"Elliot was telling me about the air-spell he's been working on. It sounds interesting! I'm surprised your father hasn't snapped him up from the Royal Guard to be a spell-maker!"

"No No, spell-making is just a hobby. I wouldn't leave the Guard. It's an honour to serve," replied Elliot.

"& it keeps you close to this handsome Prince too!" said Camila as she held Jacob's arm.

Jacob and Camila had started to become close friends ever since the Queen appointed him to the Royal Council. Although Jacob always accepted the responsibility of being heir to the throne he knew he had time to prepare for that bitter sweet day. Being on the Royal Council this soon was out of his comfort zone and Camila spotted that from day one. She took him under her wing and offered advice and how to conduct himself in the trickier more diplomatic situations. Advice he knew he would be drawing on in the coming days.

"So, I hear you're off to the White Islands to calm down the Lady Regent?" queried Camila.

"News travels fast!" replied Jacob looking slightly surprised.

"Don't worry. Your mother and I both received the demand from The Lady Regent this morning."

"I see. Yes. I leave in the morning. Any last minute advice?"

"Just keep an eye on her daughter. She's cunning. Even if her choice in men is a little questionable to say the least but you know that! Won't this be the first time you'll see Neville since he was removed from the Council?"

"Indeed it is," said Jacob rolling his eyes.

"Well, this will be fun!" smiled Elliot.

"Yes, well, we must be off. Lovely to see you Camila." Jacob and Elliot made their way out of the gardens and back down the long hallway still lined with Royal Guards and their fire spheres flickering in the air.

"So that's what your mother wanted to chat to you about? What has the Lady Regent been demanding now?" asked Elliot.

"Hmm. It appears the White Islands are now 'demanding' separation from the Empire. Mother has asked us to go and get to the bottom of it."

"She asked 'us'?"

"Well. No, she asked me but the last time I checked you are in the Prince's Guard. So you'll be coming with, naturally."

"Naturally!" Laughed Elliot.

CHAPTER THREE

THE PASSING DOME

As the sun rose casting its warm glow upon the Imperial City, Jacob stood alone staring out of his palace apartment window within the higher palace. Dressed in his black robes with gold plate armour down his right arm and the prince's crown upon his head, he turned and walked out of his rooms and began to make his way down the huge sand coloured stone staircase leading down to the Kings Hall which stood at the ground entrance of the lower palace. A huge circular hall with white banners hanging in the air with the royal crest. In the middle of this room stood an enormous golden and imposing statue of 'The First King'. It intimidated anyone visiting the Royal Palace for the first time.

Jacob walked passed the statue and out into the open courtyard passing through the gigantic stone doors guarding the entrance to the palace. Outside two of his Prince's Royal Guards waited to accompany him for the journey to the White Islands. Elliot and the other guard William stood to attention as Jacob walked towards them. Both of the guards dressed in their trademark green robes, silver helmets and golden Wielding Spears by their side.

Jacob nodded to them signifying he was ready to depart as he veered off to the right of the great courtyard with Elliot and William flanking him. They passed through a large open ivy covered stone alleyway opening up to a large sized glass dome building at the end. Four sentry guards stood side-by-side at the building entrances large glass doors.

"*Welcome to the Passing Dome, Your Highness,*" said the sentry guard.

"*Thank you,*" replied Jacob as he, Elliot and William entered the Dome.

The Passing Dome was a marvel for the eyes to behold. The only one of its kind in the world. The Dome was where you could pass to anywhere in the world through the use of 'Passing Arches'. Ten feet wide and twelve feet tall, these dark archways with shimmering light filling them scattered across the Dome. Some on the ground but most were simply floating in mid air. Jacob and his two guards made their way across the Dome.

An old kind looking lady with thin wiry grey hair came out of seemingly nowhere and walked up to Jacob bowing before him.

"*I am the caretaker of the Passing Dome, your highness. It's my understanding you wish to travel to the White Islands? That is the arch that leads to the White Island Regents Hall, gather round me closely,*" said the caretaker as she pointed to an archway high above them close to the Dome glass ceiling.

Jacob, Elliot and William came shoulder to shoulder behind the old lady. She then lifted both of her hands past her waist in-line with her shoulders and then all four of them were lifted up fifty feet through the air towards the White Islands Passing Arch. As they drew closer to the archway a stone floor appeared beneath them in front of the arch. Instinctively just enough space for the four of them to stand on. Landing softly on the stone floor the care taker reached out her palm motioning towards the archway for them to pass through. The three of them lead by Jacob walked silently through the archway to the White Islands.

Almost instantly a complete darkness was replaced by a brightening light and then shapes began to form as they exited the archway. Their eyes adjusting to the light and the smell of salty sea air filled their lungs. They had arrived on the White Islands.

CHAPTER FOUR

THE WHITE ISLANDS

Over a thousand miles off the West Coast of Ireland hundreds of small quartz coloured islands stretching over five thousands miles from north to south are the White Islands. Only a handful of the White Islands were inhabited by MagiFolk with Farland being the main island. Farland town was made up of cobbled streets curving and weaving around weather battered dark stone houses and shops. On the outskirts overlooking the town and countless islands atop a rounded hill stood the Regents Hall. The modest sized old manor surrounded by a tall and long stone circular wall was home to the The Lady Regent Catherine and her family.

The Passing Arch was at the far corner of the Regents Hall estate where Jacob, Elliot and William had just appeared. A hooded man stood in front of the archway with his arms folded to welcome them. The man pulled back his weathered hood and held out his hand to Jacob.

"Hello Kiron, it's been a long time. We are here at the request of your Lady Regent," said Jacob as he shook Kiron's hand. The blonde haired, short, well-built figure of Kiron was the youngest of Lady Regent's offspring nodded and smiled as he greeted Jacob.

"Has it? Time goes by at a slower pace out here than on the mainland. Welcome to the White Islands Prince Jacob. I'll be taking you to my mother's study where she is waiting for you," Kiron said with his accent plain. Jacob and Kiron had always managed to stay civil and respect each other throughout the turbulence Jacob found himself in with his family.

They followed Kiron through the stark grounds of wild weeds growing between the stone pathways towards the Regents Hall entrance. Jacob felt his presence was as unwelcome as the weather. Dull gray clouds loomed in the air with a brisk salty and cold wind. Kiron pushed open the manor hall doors to reveal a large entrance hall decorated with overgrown large leafed plants hanging from the walls, ceilings and between the stair banisters of the curving stairwell at the centre of the hall.

"This way," Kiron motioned them to go inside a room to the left of the hall, with the doors already open Jacob made his way in with Elliot and William closely following behind.

Inside this room was the small and slight figure of the Lady Regent. Her hair greying from what used to be blonde. She sat behind an old dark oak desk. Indeed all the pieces of furniture inside this room was of the same ageing style.

"Welcome back to the White Islands Your Highness," spoke the Lady Regent in a well spoken high pitch shrill voice which made the hairs on ones neck stand on end.

"Thank you my lady, it's as I remember it."

She offered the chair on the opposite side of her table for him to sit, he immediately obliged while Elliot and William stood several paces behind him next to the entrance holding their Wielding Spears at their side. As Jacob sat down two other people entered the room from a side entrance to the left of the Lady Regent. A very good looking woman with thick blonde hair of average height with the brightest blue eyes. A dark haired, handsome, tall muscly man followed her as they made their way to stand by either side of the Lady Regent.

"Of course you remember my daughter Kendra and her husband Neville?"

"Indeed, we are old friends," replied Jacob with a subtle and sarcastic smile.

A look fell across Neville's face of instant anger. It was obvious to Jacob the word friend was not what he would call their relationship now but his mother's words echoed in his mind for him to 'get under his skin'.

Ignoring this reaction Jacob continued to address the Lady Regent

"Lady Regent…Catherine? May I call you Catherine? I think we have all known each other long enough to drop the formalities, no?"

Catherine nodded in response

"I am here under your request to discuss these, well… worrisome demands in your own words of separation from the Empire."

Catherine let out a high pitched laugh,*"Clearly not so worrisome that the Queen sent me her son instead of coming here herself."*

"I assure you, the Queen takes this matter very seriously which is why she has sent me, the heir to the throne and with her full authority. I speak for the Queen, Catherine."

"Be that as it may, there is little to discuss, apart from your Royal Council and Queen to facilitate my demands." Catherine stared dead eyed at Jacob.

Jacob nodded and let out a long sigh,

"Surely you know it's not as simple as that. The islands are not just a place, they rest on sacred ley lines older than the

MagiFolk themselves…they hold and power the ancient barrier between us and the threat of the Dark Knights that fled to America over five hundred years ago. You cannot expect the Queen to simply 'give up' this critical strong hold because 'you' demand it". said Jacob

If it were not for the helmet on Elliot's face his expression of surprise and confusion at Jacob's comments would have been all so obvious.

"You dare attempt to educate me on the history of my islands? My family have been the regent of these islands as long as your family have been in power! Besides there hasn't been a threat from the Dark Knights in five centuries!" barked Catherine.

"Even more reason to keep the status quo," Jacob reeled calmly.

"The Empire has ignored us out here for long enough. You and your family has everything to do with that. You expect us to maintain the barrier with no reward. This is not a negotiation. I wanted the Queen to hear this directly but you'll have to do… We no longer recognise The British Empire of Magic's authority here!" said Catherine with a finality.

"And how, may I ask, do you intend to enforce this?" Jacob remaining calm but could sense the situation becoming more hostile and that Catherine had already planned for this.

"Precisely that! If it comes to it, myself, my family and the people of the White Islands and those loyal to us will enforce

our will!" Catherine shrilled in reply continuing her deathly stare at Jacob.

"A bold position to take, considering you have no army to speak of. You no longer have any influence over the Royal Council since Neville here was removed and stripped of his Royal Lordship for treason. Supplying guarded secrets to the American Republic of Magic whom are all too loyal to the Dark Knights beliefs or have you forgotten that, my lady? It would seem so as you've now invited him into your inner family circle by marrying your daughter who is to be Regent after you. I can assure you, the Queen WILL react with full force of the guard if you continue this absurd course of action." Jacob returned Catherine's dead stare with composure casting a casual glance at Neville for his reaction to his comments on him. Neville's face had flared red with anger with his fists clenched.

"If she is still Queen by the time she can give that order!" Replied an angry Neville which was clearly an unwelcome contribution to the conversation if Catherine's reaction was anything to go by but it was the very reaction Jacob was angling for.

"Do you know something I don't my old friend?" asked Jacob

"Only that it pleases me that I will live to see the Maybook dynasty destro—"

Catherine stood up and cut Neville off before he could finish his sentence.

"THAT'S ENOUGH! You have your message for the Queen. You and your guards can leave. Kiron! See them to the Passing Arch!" shouted Catherine.

Jacob rose from his chair heeding Catherines wishes.

"I fear the next time we see each other it will not be on such diplomatic terms. The Empire will not submit to your demands and as I said, there will be consequences if you take this further," said Jacob.

"A threat, Jacob?" Barked Neville.

"Merely a fact," said Jacob as he turned his back on them and followed Elliot and William lead by Kiron back into the hall and outside making their way along the stone path back to the Passing Arch.

As they stood at the front of the Passing Arch Kiron turned around to face Jacob quietly chuckling.

"You and Neville are still the closest of friends I see!" said Kiron sarcastically.

Recognising the humour in his voice and the obvious attempt at trying to defuse a tense situation Jacob joined Kiron and laughed.

"Kiron, before I leave…what did Neville mean by he would live to see my family destroyed before your mother cut him off? Clearly he said something that he shouldn't have," asked Jacob.

Kiron glanced around at their surroundings with a hint of what Jacob believed to be paranoia.

"Jacob, I like you and always have. It saddens me what has happened between our families but my mother was right about one thing…you have all forgotten us out here. As a result you underestimate her. All I can say is that she has a powerful ally, he's well hidden, but his blood line…it's old and royal. If I were you, I wouldn't regard Nevilles remarks as baseless." Kiron motioned with his hands indicating it was time for them to pass through the archway.

Jacob frowned and nodded, slightly perplexed at what Kiron had revealed to him.

"Thank you Kiron. I very much wish you well and hope that we can greet each other as friends again one day soon."

They both reached out and shared a mutual touch of their shoulders. Jacob, Elliot and William walked through the arch and as fast as they disappeared from the White Islands they re-appeared back inside the Passing Dome within the Imperial City.

CHAPTER FIVE

THE DARK KNIGHTS AND THE AMERICAN REPUBLIC OF MAGIC

Jacob, Elliot and William exited the Passing Dome and Elliot quickened his pace to come up next to Jacob and grabbed his wrist pulling Jacob to a stop. They looked at each other and Jacob knew what this was about and he knew there was no ignoring it… Elliot needed answers about the The Dark Knights. Jacob turned to look at William.

"William, thank you for accompanying me today, that'll be all you may take the rest of the day for yourself," Jacob motioned William back down the ivy covered alleyway towards the Royal Palace.

"As you wish your highness, thank you," said William as he left the two of them in the middle of the alleyway.

"Jacob, What wa-" started Elliot but Jacob cut him off.

"Yes, I know. Look there is a bench seat over there by the lake. Let's just go sit and talk. You can take that helmet off now, you're off duty," said Jacob lovingly as they walked towards

the large open lake with oak trees covering the edges providing shade from the summer sun over the benches beneath them. They sat down at the nearest bench and Jacob let Elliot ask the questions he'd been burning to ask since he heard Jacob speak of the Dark Knights.

"What just happened over there?" asked Elliot.

"Well, a few things happened over there didn't they?! But I assume you are referring to that business about the Dark Knights?"

"Yes! You were speaking as if they still exist? You all were! But they died out after the Magi War?"

"Well…The Dark Knights may have died out but their beliefs live on in what has now become the American Republic of Magic and their intense hate and dislike of the Human world has always put us at odds with them."

Elliot nodded perplexed his blonde hair messy from wearing his helmet. Jacob continued, shrugging his shoulders.

"As you know, about eight hundred years ago the Magi Wars broke out between all the magical kingdoms which lasted for two hundred years. Two sides. One side that wanted to wage a war on the human world which were lead by the Dark Knights as everyone knows and the other side, which were lead by 'The Bonum' who believed we could coexist with humans by obscuring us from them using our magic. So they fought and they fought and it almost pushed our kind to extinction but ultimately 'The Bonum' won and forced The Dark Knights or at

least the ones that survived into exile across the great ocean to the furthest land which we now know as America. Which is where the White Islands are introduced into this little history lesson. Because these Dark Knights were so powerful even just the few that remained, 'The Bonum' created two barriers using ancient ley lines. The first barrier in China, The Great Wall in fact and the second…The White Islands. These two barriers stopped The Dark Knights or any magical being crossing over to our side from their exile in America unless of course they had royal permission, which is how it has been for the last five hundred years."

Jacob studied Elliot's overwhelming expression of concentration. As he opened his mouth to ask another question Jacob raised his hand to stop him,

"One of the most important parts of that period of history is also one of the worst kept secrets of our Empire… What most do not know is that the leader and most powerful member of The Dark Knights was non other than King Colet of The British Empire of Magic. Yes. Not exactly a piece of history we are proud of but he was deposed and exiled to America with the rest of them when the war ended five hundred years ago," continued Jacob. Elliot's bright blue eyes stared out into the lake until the thought that Jacob had been waiting for him to realise had struck him.

"Five hundred years ago King Colet was deposed? That's when the first Maybook came to the throne. Straight after Colet?" said Elliot as he turned to look at Jacob.

"Yes, it was my ancestor Royal Lord Acca May-book that lead the coup that deposed King Colet. He then succeeded him to become King Acca Maybook, the first of the Maybooks…hence his big golden statue in the Great Hall. Maybe you've seen it?" said Jacob laughing sarcastically.

"Wow, that's a lot of new information." said Elliot

"Well it's old information actually, but new to you…don't worry, you've got time to digest it! I have to go to my mother and deliver the Lady Regent's message," said Jacob as he stood up from the bench and straightened his robes and thick dark hair.

"What were you and Kiron talking about before we left?" asked Elliot as Jacob was about to walk away.

"Hopefully nothing of importance! I'll see you later," said Jacob as Elliot stood up. They kissed briefly and Jacob walked back to the Royal Palace to see his mother, leaving Elliot by the lake.

As Jacob was walking back into the courtyard in front of the Great Hall Entrance to the Royal Palace he knew that what this ally of the White Islands Kiron was warning him about was definitely 'important and worrying'. His mother needed to know at once.

CHAPTER SIX

MAGIWOLF

Meanwhile, deep in the highland mountains of Scotland, MagiFolk of the sleepy village of Colghorn went about their day. This village was small and quaint with only one pub called 'The King's Crest' which had its regulars night after night.

All the MagiFolk knew each other with many families living there generation after generation. Their lives were solitary apart from the occasional visit of students or teachers coming from the nearby Royal Guard training facility a few miles south.

The local Spell Master Henry was taking his daily walk down to the bakery to pick up the bread for his wife and sons. Henry was a tall man with a fair amount of gut ahead of him. Something that had been hard earned at the King's Crest over the last few decades. As Henry approached the bakery he heard the sounds of a POP! as loud as a gunshot. He stopped instantly with his hand on the door handle.

Another POP! instantly followed by the bloodcurdling screams of a woman from the way Henry had walked down. He turned on his heel and ran as fast as his lungs and heavy legs could manage. As he ran up the cobbled street drawing closer to the location he had heard the screams another POP!

came from the other side of the village, this time he heard a man's voice shouting…

"RUN! EVERYONE, GET INSIDE!"

Henry heard an even louder POP! but this time it was from right behind him. He turned around facing a dark tiny street with tall houses on either side. The street was too dark to see anything but a strange dark grey mist started spilling out onto the street. He drew in closer with his hands raised palms out in front of him. A low pitched growl started to fill his ears followed by a damp and sodden smell. As he peered closer into the street, two red eyes peered back narrowing in on him. Henry knew this was no dog. Suddenly the red eyes of this animal came closer out into the daylight of the street revealing itself. A huge wolf-like animal stood there, its teeth drawn and with its hairless muscled body tensed as if ready to leap for Henry's throat at any moment. Somehow Henry remained calm, his breathing steady and his mind focused to cast a powerful spell if needed and just as he took one step backwards the wolf-like beast leaped into the air towards Henry. Fire erupted from Henrys palms and engulfed the beast with a spiral of flames. The animal let out a screeching howl followed by another POP! and the beast had disappeared with the flames still roaring Henry then sensed another figure in the shadows but not a wolf, it was a man. Henry pulled the flames back into perfect spheres above each of his palms. The man dressed in a dirty old cloak dropped to his knees slammed his hands on the floor. The ground began to shake and exploded in front of Henry sending the sharpest pieces of stone and rock towards him. Once again in fear for his life Henry threw the spheres of fire towards the cloaked figure obliterating the shards of lethal rock and stone eventually the fire balls hurtled into the figure knocking the man backwards into the ground unconscious.

Henry fell to the floor in relief and shock, his ears ringing. He quickly tried to centre himself as he could start to hear the sounds of more POPs! and screams from all corners of the village. He looked up and saw a woman rushing down the street towards him screaming his name carrying a young boy in her arms. Blood covering her white gown he could see his wife and youngest son. Henry's family had been attacked.

CHAPTER SEVEN

THE OLD RETURN

The Queen paced her grand sized apartment floor back and forth in the higher palace murmuring to herself. Her hair tied back dressed in an old military style jacket and long robes over the top. Her guard had informed her that Jacob had returned from the White Islands and was on his way to see her. A firm bang on her apartment stone doors preceded the royal guard entering the room with Jacob following behind him.

"*Jacob! Good you're here. There have been developments since you've been gone and a Royal Council meeting was held.*" The Queen continued to pace the room as she spoke.

Jacob raised his eyebrows at his mother. He was clearly worried at her unease. As the guard left, Jacob raised his arm in the air and flicked his hand closing the stone doors behind. With the loud thud the doors were closed and it was just the two of them.

"*Blimey, I've only been gone a for the day! What happened that warranted a Royal Council meeting?*"

"*We'll get to that… What have you learned from the islands?*"

"*Nothing good. As far as they are concerned they've separated from the Empire with immediate effect. In her Lady Regent' own words which are meant to be delivered to you via myself 'We no longer recognise The British Empire of Magic's authority here!' and it was said with much finality.*
I of course relayed the consequences of this action towards the Empire could invoke a military response. Of which she seemed unfazed by. Probably because she's found herself an ally, so it was revealed to me by her son Kiron no-less after an initial outburst from Neville."

The Queen stopped her pacing and looked straight at Jacob. "*An ally?*"

"Yes, apparently he's powerful and has a royal bloodline to-boot, according to Kiron anyway."

"Royal? Did Kiron give you any idea what royal blood line he belonged to?" the Queen spoke as she sat in a large white fabric covered chair by a window in the corner of the room.

"No. Sorry," Jacob replied lowering his head

"Don't be, you did very well my son. This information is valuable, especially in light of the current happenings in the North." Jacob looked at her confused.

"We have received reports of Magiwolf attacks in the North of the country. In two separate locations. A Royal Guard training facility and at Colghorn village just north of the facility."

"Magiwolf? What!? There hasn't been a sighting for centuries!"

Jacob instantly flashed back to a history lesson during his school days when he was boy. A passage from a book that he could recite word for word that described the Magiwolf gave him nightmares for months.

"The MagiWolfs were the creature of choice used by the Dark Knights in the Magi Wars. Sharp toothed and completely hairless wolf-like animals with short-range teleportation abilities made them extremely dangerous even against powerful *sorcerers. Once their bite was inflicted a venom that was so deadly and swift the victim would be dead within minutes"*

"There hasn't been a confirmed sighting for three hundred years in fact. With the news you've brought back from the White Islands and these attacks…it's more than just coincidence that this is all happening at the same time," said the Queen.

"Do you think the Lady Regent is behind the attacks?" asked Jacob

"Not solely. Catherine isn't bold enough to act on her own so these attacks, I would assume are the work of her mystery ally"

"What about the Guard facility?" Jacob interrupted

The Queen looked at him with a grave and sad expression *"Apart from a handful of trainees and teachers that made it through the Passing Arch in time…everyone was slaughtered."*

"Why do this to us? If it's a war the White Islands want then attacking our Guard facility is one thing but a village full of innocent MagiFolk? It's outrageous!" demanded Jacob.

The Queen sighed stood up from her chair and walked over to him,
"My son. Whoever planned this attack will feel the full force of this Empire's wrath but assumptions are a dangerous thing. No one has claimed responsibility for the attacks yet. This instils confusion and fear which is undoubtedly the goal of whoever is behind it. So…we have to find out who this ally of the Lady

Regent's is. My instinct is that this is where our greatest threat lies which is why I want you to go with Royal Lady Kerr to Colghorn and see what you can find out and who lead the attack. Our knowledge of the MagiWolfs have degraded over the years but as far as we can gather they do not act without a master. Which is why the Dark Knights used them so effectively during the Great Wars. In the meantime I will go to our Parliament and inform them of the situation. They represent the people and if these attacks escalate we will need all of our forces united."

Jacob held is mother and hugged her close. It was true that their relationship was a powerful bond between mother and son before anything else.

"I understand mother. When is Camila expecting me?" and just as Jacob asked the question there was the familiar bang on the apartment stone door.

"Yes, enter,". replied the Queen.

The Royal Guard opened the doors and Royal Lady Camila Kerr stood in the door way with a warm smile dressed in a long brown and thick fur robe, her blonde wavy hair resting on the tightly wrapped furry collar of her robe.

"You can expect me now your highness…these doors aren't as thick as you think!" said Camila with a soft chuckle in her voice indicating she overheard Jacob and his mother's conversation.

"Oh the doors are fine, Camila. It's just your talent for knowing and hearing things others simply cannot is still as sharp as ever," replied the Queen with a warm smile. *"which is why I am always happy you're on my side"*

"Always, your majesty," replied Camila. *"There is a platoon of guards in the courtyard awaiting us, Jacob. We best be on our way."* Jacob smiled as his mother and held her arm.

"Good luck with Parliament. We will find out what we can at Colghorn," said Jacob and he left his mother and joined Camila to leave the higher palace and back down to the courtyard.

As they walked out through the Kings Hall and into the courtyard Jacob could see the platoon of a hundred or more Royal Guards standing in a perfect square formation. Camila pulled back on Jacob's arm to her side *"I hope you don't mind but I had Elliot reassigned just for today to be out onto your mother's guard for her visit to Parliament. He's one of the most gifted sorcerers in the guard as you know and I want her protected".*

"You think someone may try and attack her at Parliament?" Jacob asked worryingly.

"Jacob, these are uncertain times. I simply want her protected with our best."

"Of course, mother trusts him also," Jacob nodded in a agreement.

"Good! They've prepared the widened Passing Arch to be brought here in the courtyard. It'll take us directly to Colghorn."

Behind the platoon of Royal Guards, four sorcerers using air spells guided a huge Passing Arch through the air under the watchful eye of the old lady caretaker. As it rested gently on the ground before them the Passing Arch came to life with its shimmering light filling the darkened archway creating the passage to Colghorn.

Camila and Jacob walked ahead of the platoon and stood at the threshold of the Passing Arch. Camila turned to Jacob and spoke quietly,

"I suggest you prepare yourself for what we may see on the other side. Reports of the attacks have been savage and without discrimination."

Jacob took a deep breath and subtly nodded his head, they walked through the arch with the platoon marching behind.

CHAPTER EIGHT

COLET! COLET! COLET!

As soon as Jacob passed through the arch his senses became overwhelmed. Cries of despair invaded his ears, smoke filled his lungs and the chaos of seeing the villagers running out from houses with rags covered in blood and fire in the streets.

As Jacob turned around to see the guard coming through the Colghorn Passing Arch he noticed it had no stone archway but just the shimmering light floating in a huge semi circle out of the ground.

Camila turned to command the platoon and the guards were clearly startled by what they were witnessing at the village.

"Guards! Division one set a defence perimeter around the village. Division two help the wounded and set up the hospital tent. Division three put the fires out!" Camila commanded the platoon with an experienced flair of control and calm.

As the divisions parted off an older lady limped up to where Jacob and Camila were standing. Her face dirtied with blood and tears in her eyes she fell to the ground with Camila catching the lady in her arms.

"Please help us! It was MagiWolfs, I swear it. They've killed so many. Children!!! THEY KILLED OUR CHILDREN!" she cried.

"We are here to help. We've brought the Royal Guard who are trained medically to help your wounded and to protect you from the MagiWolf. Can you tell me where I can find your Spell Master?" Camila held the old lady as if it were her own mother.

"Henry? Yes yes. He's at the King's Crest, it's where we are taking the dead. He'll be there, his youngest boy was bitten," said the lady through tears.

"Thank you". Camila beckoned over a couple of the guards who rushed over to them at once.
"Take care of this lady and see to her wounds."
The guards helped the old lady off the ground and carried her away to where the guards were setting up a makeshift hospital tent in the corner of the village centre. Camila stood up and turned to Jacob,

"Let's find this Spell Master!"

The two of them made their way through the village streets where by now the guard were hard at work helping the wounded and calming the chaos.

Jacob and Camila arrived outside the King's Crest. The hanging sign swung eerily above the door which was ajar. Jacob pushed opened the door revealing a scene of dozens of fatally wounded and lifeless bodies from MagiWolf attacks laying on the pub tables and floors. Villagers were using tables cloths and even their own robes to cover the bodies of those that had passed away. As Camila and Jacob made their way further into the pub the villagers halted their actions as it was obvious from the way they were dressed they were from the Royal Council. Camila looked down at the lifeless body covered in cloth nearest her and then she spoke to the villagers staring at her and Jacob.

"My name is Royal Lady Kerr and this is Prince Jacob. We've come to help. There is a hospital tent being setup in your village centre. I will send for guards to help with those that have passed on and organise any arrangements that are required."
A murmuring of acknowledgement and some audible 'thank yous' came in reply from the villagers.

"We were told that your Spell Master, Henry is among you here?" continued Camila.

One of the men pointed towards the far corner of the

pub, *"He's over there. He's just lost his youngest son my lady,"* said the man softly in a thick Scottish accent.

"Thank you," replied Camila as she and Jacob made their way over to Henry.

He stood hunched over the table in the furthest corner, his own robes lay covering the small shape of the figure of his son underneath.

"I am so sorry for your loss," said Camila softly, standing behind him.

Henry turned around to face Camila and Jacob, his eyes red and swollen as he looked at Jacob

"You're the Queens boy no?" in his deep Scottish but grief stricken voice.

"I am sir and I am so sorry for what has happened here," replied Jacob.

Henry nodded and turned back around to continuing his stare at the table.

"Henry, I am sorry to ask this of you now but time is not on our side and I was told that you fought one of the beasts and alerted the Royal Council of the attack?" said Camila.

"Aye. Couldn't believe what I was seeing but, aye, a MagiWolf it was and its master who I reckon you'd wanna be speaking to no?" Henry spoke without breaking from his stare at the table. Camila took a step forward closer to Henry.

"Its master? You saw its master?" Camila said completely surprised.

"Aye, tried to kill me too after I did away with the MagiWolf. He's down in the cellar. Got a couple of the lads keeping an n eye on him until you lot arrived."

"He's here, alive?" Jacob interjected.

"He's in and out of consciousness but he'll be coming round by now I'd be reckoning. Behind the bar down the stairs. You'll find him."

"Henry, thank you. I am so sorry to invade your privacy at this terrible moment. Anything we can do to help just ask for me," said Camila as she beckoned Jacob with her head towards the bar.

"He's been saying your name a lot, your highness," said Henry to Jacob as they were walking away.

Jacob nodded at at Henry and he and Camila made their way behind the bar and through a small stoney passageway down some stairs lit with fire-lanterns. The smell of ale and whisky filled their noses as they reached a small metal gate. Camila pushed open the gate with a noisy creak they entered a darkly lit cavern underneath the pub filled with ale barrels. In the centre of the cavern two villagers stood either side of a dark robed figure laying still on the ground. His hands bound in glowing blue chains behind his back. One of the villager's saw the royal crest on Jacob's arms, the gold glistening in the dim fire light.

"Prince Jacob? Your highness!" both the villagers bowed their heads to Jacob.

"Thank you Gentlemen. this is the MagiWolfs master?" said Jacob.

"That's what we think your highness. We've got him in a binding spell after Henry knocked him out."

"Has he showed signs regaining consciousness yet?" asked Camila.

"Just started to my lady. He's been groaning and moving a little," said the villager.

"Alright, thank you both. You can leave him with us down here for a little while," said Camila.

Both of the villagers looked at each other with concern.

"Are you sure my lady? From what Henry said he's pretty dangerous."

"So are we," said Camila as she looked at both the villagers squarely. Jacob stood aside making room for the two men to leave. They left without another word making their way back up to the pub.

Camila knelt down closer to the chained figure and pulled back the hood covering his head. A scarred face of a man what looked to be in his mid fifties his eyelids starting to move and began to open. Grunting softly and he rolled onto his back his eyes open. Camila stood up and looked down at him.

"Who are you?" asked Camila sternly, staring into his eyes.

The man looked up twisting his head in an attempt to get a clearer look at Camila. He smiled at her with his blooded teeth showing and sinister laugh echoing through the cavern. His eyes darting to Jacob and his laugh grew louder.

"Royal Lady Kerr and the Queen's son! He'd said you'd come!" said the man while coughing and spitting blood. neither Camila or Jacob fazed by his words.

"Oh we know who we are but it's you I want to know about. Who said we'd come? Who do you answer to?" said Camila. The man rolled back onto his front his face on the ground and dirt.

"My mind is his. A vessel for his commands."

"I see. Well, let's find out what secrets you hold in your mind."

Camila raised her right hand out and flicked her fingers back into her palm. With that the man flew up off the floor and into the air, head height with Camila, suspended in mid-air. The man groaned in pain. Jacob eyes narrowed questioning what Camila was planning. She placed both her hands on the man's temples. The man cried out in agony.

"HE IS THE TRUE KING! MY LIFE IS HIS!" cried out the man. Jacob strode forward next to Camila.

"What is he saying?" Camila eyes closed in concentration ignoring Jacob.

"It cannot be!...show me everything!" bellowed Camila. The man's cry grew louder, his eyes wide open staring up at the ceiling and then darting from left to right like he was speed reading a book. His feet shaking uncontrollably. Jacob turned his head as this was getting harder and more painful to watch but then the man began shouting a name over and over again that made Jacob snap back.

"COLET! COLET! COLET!"

The man's cries were now hard to decipher between pain and jubilation as blood started running from his nose Camila opened her eyes in shock of what she had seen in the man's mind and lifted her hands from the his temples breaking the mind spell. The man fell to the ground barely alive, quivering in pain.

Camila stumbled backwards breathing heavily as the two village men came running back into the cavern.

"Call for the guard...bring them here to us" said Camila breathlessly to the two village men who were still standing still trying to take in what was going on in the cavern

"NOW!" shouted Camila.

The village men ran back up the stairs in search for the guard.

"Camila, what just happened?" asked Jacob. Camila shook her head looking at the collapsed man on the ground.

"They're here. Just north of the village through the woods. An old ruined castle." Camila now looked over at Jacob who was staring at her confused and in need of answers.

"Who? Camila! What did you see?"

"MagiWolves and their masters. Hundreds of them, maybe a thousand even…and they left him here as a message…for you Jacob" Camila clearly startled and still catching her breath she looked back down at the MagiWolf master on the ground.

"For me?" said Jacob confused. Camila looked up at Jacob with worry.

"Yes. It seems the leader of this MagiWolf army wants to speak with you," said Camila.

"Who is he? Did you see him?"

"It was just his name that echoed in the man's mind that was intended for you to hear…it was Thomas Colsom."

"Thomas? As in my friend when I was a boy? Thats impossible. He died along with his family. Twenty years ago! They were murdered."

"They were. But Thomas's body was never found."

"He's alive!?" Jacob was confused, relieved and shocked all at the same time. His pulse was racing. He didn't know what to think

 "Alive and in command of a MagiWolf army it would seem."

Rushed foot steps echoed from the stairwell as two royal guards appeared in the cavern with the village men. Camila composed herself and began to walk towards the guards *"Stand guard over this man. No one else is to come down here".* Commanded Camila.

Her and Jacob made their way back up into the pub where the dead had been cleared from the room. Jacob turned to Camila *"Camila, where did you see that Thomas wants to meet with me?"*

"No Jacob. You are not to meet with this man. We have no idea what he plans to do or how dangerous he is!"

"All due respects Camila, know your place! If I wish to meet with this person who claims to be one of my oldest friends who I believed to be dead for the last twenty years…then I will!" snapped Jacob

Camila bowed her head slightly breaking the eye contact between them

"And it could be a trap, Jacob," said Camila

"If what you said is true and he has that many numbers of MagiWolf and masters just a few miles north then we are vastly outnumbered. If I meet with him, it will buy you enough time to send for enough guards to fight this. It sounds to me as if this castle they are held up in could be a stronghold of some sort. We could end this as quickly as it started." Camila looked back at Jacob knowing he spoke sense but the risk he would be taking was huge.

"Just east of the village there is a large tree, a small lake. That's all I saw…but you MUST take a company of guards with you and I will return by the end of the day with an army of Royal Guard."

"One last thing before I leave, Camila. Why was that man shouting the name Colet?" asked Jacob

"That, I truly do not know. The memory it was coming from was blurred but powerful."

CHAPTER NINE

TRUTH OR DYNASTY

Darkness had now fallen over the town of Colghorn with the moon shining full across the land and mountains in the distance. Jacob along with four royal guards were making their way along the frozen muddy path towards the lake to the east of the village. The directions from Camila were simple enough.

"Just through the woodland to the east you'll find Colghorn Lake on the other side."

Jacob's heart hadn't stopped racing since he heard Thomas' name. A name he hadn't heard aloud in two decades. He began to cast his mind back to his childhood as he walked and every memory Jacob had of Thomas was fond. From growing up together their family homes neighboured each other, hidden away from the human eye along the picturesque south west coast of England. They would see each other almost everyday, practising spells together. As they got a little older Thomas' magic was growing more and more impressive always matching Jacob's ability. Thomas' ability was surprising as he came from an ordinary family with no magical talents to remark of in fact, the only reason that he and Thomas were friends was because his father was an accomplished architect and had been commissioned by Jacob's grandfather to design countless buildings for the Imperial City and was gifted a residence within the royal coastal estate where Jacob lived with his mother and father until Jacob's 13th birthday when Thomas and his family had disappeared.

   "Your highness, I think this must be the lake," said the guard closest to Jacob.

   He quickly snapped his mind back into the present looking out across the lake. The full moon reflecting off its glassy and still surface. A tall tree to the left of the lake stood on its own. Jacob began to motion towards the path surrounding the lakes edge. The guards followed him but Jacob held out his hand to stop them.

   "Stay here. I must go alone."

   "Your highness Royal Lady Kerr ordered us not to leave your side," replied the concerned guard.

Jacob smiled at the guard, *"Well, I out rank her so I'm ordering you to stay here. Don't worry, I am more than capable of looking after myself,"* he said winking at the guard and Jacob continued along the path toward the lonesome tree on his own.

As Jacob approached the tree he felt the air change and vibrate. He knew straight away it was a masking spell. The very same type of spell used to hide towns and cities of MagiFolk from human eyes. Jacob knew this was powerful magic, he also knew it was Thomas' magic.

From behind the tree Jacob heard faint footsteps as a dark hooded figure silhouetted in the moonlight stepped out in front of him.

"You finally got that growth spurt then?"

The silhouetted figure pulled back his hood and as he spoke and stepped closer as Jacob stepped back cautiously. Jacob studied his face. Even in the poor light of the moon he could recognise it was Thomas. His thin face and prominent jawline with pale green eyes stared right into Jacob's.

"It is you. I can't believe it. After all this time…Thomas?"

Jacob now stepped a little closer to Thomas as he looked back over his shoulder at the royal guards who stood where he left them. Thomas pointed to the masking spell where the air shimmered slightly and smiled, *"Don't worry about them,* all they see is you standing here on your own," said Thomas. Jacob smiled and shook his head at Thomas.

"Masking spell? Impressive," said Jacob.

"I've had time to improve," replied Thomas.

"What is all this Thomas? Did you attack that village and the training facility? Why?"

Thomas breathed in deeply as he stared at Jacob.

"There is so much you don't know Jacob. So much that has been hidden from you. About our families and how we are fated together. Tell me…what do you think happened to me, my mother and father?"

"What I was told…what everyone was told, that extremists broke into the Royal Estate trying to get to the Kings family but your family were attacked instead. I was told you all died, Thomas."

Thomas walked a couple of meters over and knelt down at the lakes edge, his reflection staring back at him with Jacob standing behind him.

"Yes that was the story told and created by the Royal Council and your mother. What everyone believed so readily… A lie nevertheless. Told to protect your family and your claim to the throne. The truth however is that the King, your grandfather murdered my mother and father for their name and the threat

it meant to his crown." Jacob walked round to the side of Thomas to look at him as Thomas stood up.

"You're insane, Thomas! You're accusing my grandfather of killing your parents? My mother for covering it up and for what? Your name? Your father was an architect! Thomas this makes no sense."

"That's precisely what your grandfather thought when I started displaying exceptional talent for spell casting. You must remember when we were around eleven or twelve? You and I would often have spell cast-offs. I would always match your ability and strength. More often than not win the cast-offs." Thomas spoke with a slight smile remembering these moments but Jacob was still dazed and confused at what he was saying.

Thomas continued, *"Well…your grandfather and my father were equally surprised by my abilities. The King was determined to find out my family's lineage as a result…as you know my father always said we came from a perfectly common family and he genuinely believed that…your grandfather however, didn't. After all, how could a low-born boy possess such magical power?"* Said Thomas sarcastically raising his eyebrows.

"I always thought you were just gifted?" Jacob interrupted. Thomas smiled at Jacob and tilted his head.

"You always were a good kid and a little naive Jacob…But as it turned out your grandfather was right to investigate my bloodline…you see my father wasn't born here in England. No, in fact he was born in the American Republic of Magic which we

all knew, but what we didn't know is that he descended from a long line of powerful sorcerers dating back to the age of the first kings of the British Empire of Magic with an ancient claim to the throne but they were banished to the American lands centuries ago...I suppose you know what they called those people, Jacob?"

"*The Dark Knights,*" said Jacob plainly. A silence had fallen around them, not even the wind whispered. Both their breaths forming condensation mist as they exhaled in the freezing cold night.

"*Yes, exactly. You see Jacob my true family name isn't Colsom. No, it was changed to that to protect the secret but over the centuries even my own family had lost the truth about our bloodline.*" A silence grew further between them as they stared at each other. Somehow Jacob instinctively knew the name Thomas was about to utter...

"*My true name is Thomas Colet. I am the last living royal blood descendent of King Colet, leader of The Dark Knights.*"

"*If that were even true! If your father was who you say he was, how could he pass through the barrier from America? It won't allow any magical being through, especially a Dark Knight descendent!*" exclaimed Jacob.

"*Unless it's by royal invitation. Like you said, my father was the Kings architect. Your grandfather unwittingly invited a Dark Knight to his Empire,*" replied Thomas.

Jacob shook his head and turned around as if to leave but he just stood frozen still with his back to Thomas. His eyes searching the ground as if there were answers to be found growing from the mud and tree roots beneath him. He didn't want to hear anymore but he had to know more.

"So my grandfather found out your were of royal blood?" Jacob asked keeping his back turned to Thomas.

"Yes. That night, just before your birthday in fact, for a change I left your place earlier than normal.. Mum always had a go at me for never making it back in time for dinner so I thought I would be on time for once. When I got home I saw the King and my parents talking in our living room. I stayed out of sight and listened in on the conversation. Strange, even though you and I shared so much time together you'd think I would be used to the royal family but when it was the King wow! I was in awe of him."

Thomas acted out his emotion of seeing the king by throwing is hands in the air gleefully,

"Anyway, they began to argue. After it had been revealed who we were and what it meant to the establishment my father demanded the rights that came with the name. Not for himself you see, for me. He said to the King that I should be given a place on the Royal Council when I came of age just like his grandson Jacob. I was so proud of my father in that moment but the King didn't take too kindly to it. What happened next is still so fragmented in my mind but, I remember that my father didn't stand a chance against the power of the King. My father was dead before he hit the ground and my mother…my mother ran out of that room as fast as she could, I take some solace in the thought that she was running to find me but she didn't *make it out of that room either. I saw both my parents lying lifeless on the floor, killed by the man I idolised. I knew I would be next if he could find me so I ran...and I didn't stop running. My first thought was to find you but I knew that was a death sentence for me so with what knowledge of magic I had I used to change my appearance and hid away in the human world until now."*

Jacob had now turned around facing Thomas with pure dismay across his face. Jacob felt dazed and in shock. He couldn't believe Thomas's words, he wouldn't. Angry Jacob walked up face to face with Thomas with fury in his eyes.

"You expect me to believe this? How dare you accuse my family of thisThomas! You and I were friends, closer than friends! We were like brothers! You think I would believe that one of our Empires most loved Kings was capable of murdering two people in cold blood? I won't. You made a mistake coming here Thomas. You may have tricked this army of MagiWolves you've somehow amassed but it will be defeated and you WILL be arrested. You're the only murderer in this story, Thomas. This is why you asked to meet with me? To tell me this illusion of a story?" Jacob was so consumed by anger and caught up in the emotion that he was spitting the last few words in Thomas's face but Thomas just took a few steps back and straightened himself after Jacob's outburst.

"I asked you here to stop a war, Jacob. I could've given the order to attack the village as soon as you and the Royal Lady Kerr arrived with the Royal Guard but I want to give you the chance to join me and avoid the bloodshed.

The humans have been left unchecked for too long. They poison our skies and pollute our oceans. Their population grows as ours is pushed further and further into the shadows. We can fix all that... Together we can right the wrongs of the past. Rule as one. Bring down an Empire built on lies and deception that you've been subject to just as much as myself!"

"You plan to wage a war on your own kind just so you can fight the human world? You're going to need a lot more than a MagiWolf army, Thomas!"

"That army is just the beginning Jacob. In a matter of hours I will have control over the White Island barrier and the forces that have pledged to me on the other side. After your grandfather killed my parents I didn't crawl into a dark hole and lick my wounds, Jacob. No... I heard enough of that conversation between the King and my parents to know that there were people that would remember the Colet name in the American Republic of Magic loyal to The Dark Knights and their beliefs. I have amassed a big enough force to take on this so-called Empire of Magic and win, Jacob. I don't expect you to turn your back on your family on my word. What I expect you to do is simple...ask your mother... Ask her if what I said is true."

Jacob in that moment felt true fear strike his core for the first time today. Jacob wouldn't believe what Thomas was saying but the thought of asking his mother and if it were true. What would he do? Jacob's mind was racing and Thomas could sense it.

Thomas held out a red coloured jagged crystal in his hand.

"From what I have learnt, neither your mother or the Royal Council know of my lineage. This is a Blood Crystal. It contains my memory of that night my parents were killed by your grandfather. As you know, Blood Crystals cannot be falsified. Give it to your mother. I will give you until tomorrow afternoon…three o clock… Tell her forces to surrender to me… for her to abdicate and in return, I will spare her life and allow you to co-rule with me."

"Is that all?" Jacob replied laughing angrily at him. "Thomas, this won't happen. I refuse to believe any of this."

"It's time for us to part our ways for now my old friend. When you know I speak the truth, ask yourself who can you really trust?"

"And what will you do if we don't agree to your terms?"

Thomas backed away from Jacob and turned to walk away and spoke one last word before disappearing into the darkness.

"War," he said finally. Jacob stood alone and cold in the night air.

CHAPTER TEN

SHATTERED TRUTHS

Jacob and his company of guards made their way back up the main street into the Colghorn village square. The moon was giving way to the rise of a new sun throwing its warm red glow across the Highland mountains with the stillness from the evening still in the air. As he drew closer to the village square that stillness was broken by a murmuring and what sounded like a large crowd gathering. Jacob turned the corner and into the large open space of the village square that had now been completely filled with two thousand royal guards all standing in full uniform and wielding spears. Overwhelmed by what he saw and realised Royal Lady Kerr had made good on her word and brought back an army big enough to take on the MagiWolf threat.

Camila appeared from the crowd of guards walking towards Jacob flanked by two of her guards.

"Jacob! Thank goodness. Your mother has been worried. She's waiting for you. We've set up a temporary command centre at the King's Crest."

Jacob nodded but didn't say a word in reply. He simply turned and made his way back along the street to the King's Crest. Camila followed him with both their guard details forming into one. The entrance to the King's Crest was now guarded by two of the Queen's Guard, their robes black and helmets gold. Their wielding spears crossed to block the door. They bowed to Jacob and uncrossed their spears and the door flew open. As he walked into the room he could see that it had been completely transformed. The tables had gone, replaced by one large circular table in the centre of the room with a crowd of military men and woman all discussing operations and pointing to a map that lay across the table. Miniature mountains, rivers and the village itself rose out of the map in lifelike three dimensional reality. The Royal Guard Army in the middle of the village and the MagiWolf army just north.

Jacob could see his mother at the rear of the room talking with a tall man wearing deep green and tight fitted military clothing. Every item of clothing on her shouted power and command. Deep black tight fitted trousers and gold studded top with her right arm completely covered in gold armour. A dark green long flowing robe was fur lined and swept the floor. Laying Majestically on her thick wavy dark hair her golden crown.

He marched over to her barging through three of the people studying the map on his way with Camila close following behind him. Jacob pushed himself in front of his mother, putting his back to the tall military man. He stared into his mothers eye's squarely.

"We need to talk, alone. Now!" said Jacob.

The Queen blinked very slowly and turned towards the rest of the room *"Clear the room, please."*

With the Queen's command the military men and women around the table exited the room leaving just Royal Lady Kerr, Jacob and The Queen.

Jacob looked at Camila *"I meant alone."*

The Queen glanced over at Camila and beckoned her to leave with a nod of her head. Camila, bowed and went out side.

Now Jacob and The Queen were completely alone in the pub. The two stared at each other for a few minutes before Jacob walked over and sat down beside where his mother stood.

"The guards told me that this so-called Thomas Colsom didn't turn up after all?" said the Queen.

"Oh he did," the Queen looked confused,*"masking spell,"* Jacob continued plainly.

The Queen raised her eyes and sat down next to Jacob. *"Impressive."*

"That's what I said," nodded Jacob.

He looked at his mother for the first time asking if he really knew her at all. What if she admits what Thomas told him was true? What would he do? How would he react. He honestly didn't know.

The Queen smiled back at him lowering her head.

"I see. So it is him. That complicates things, doesn't it?" she said knowingly.

Jacob reached into the pocket of his robes and pulled out the Blood Crystal and passed it to his mother. She frowned as she looked down at it.

"A Blood Crystal? His?" asked the Queen. Jacob simply nodded in reply.

She took the crystal from his hand and placed her other hand over the top and closed her eyes. The memory within the crystal revealed its self to her. She relived Thomas' traumatic memory of the night his parents were murdered by her father and the shocking truth of why. She saw everything in his memory in the third person as if she was hovering ghost-like. She reopened her eyes as the memory finished. She dropped the crystal out of her hands letting it fall on the floor making Jacob jump. She stood up and stepped backwards her eyes looked on the floor where the crystal fell. Jacob looked up at her, his eyes filling up.

"It's true then? Everything he told me. It's true? And you knew all along?" He asked as his voice was breaking and wavering under the intense emotions he was feeling. Was it anger, sadness or disappointment? He didn't know.

"I didn't know who he really was but yes I knew the King was responsible for taking their lives. I believed all three of them dead until now. I never knew why. the King refused to tell me why. It's haunted me ever since" Said the Queen.

Jacob stood up to face his mother, a single tear falling from his left eye. *"And you covered it up? You and the Royal Council hid the truth from the world to protect yourselves!"*

"Your grandfather, my father, died for his crimes Jacob! By my own hand I took his life for what he did. If we had let the truth out, there would be civil war, not to mention that our enemies would have taken advantage which would have lead us to an inevitable war. We did what...I did what had to be done to protect ourselves and our people. The people loved their King, I loved him! This... the truth...would have shattered all of his achievements."

The tears fell fast from the Queen's eyes. Even though his anger was brimming the sight of his mother crying which he'd never seen in his life before, overwhelmed him. He wanted to comfort and hug her but he still felt too much anger and disappointment.

"He's asked you to surrender," said Jacob as she, the queen, his mother straightened herself as if to shake off the emotions she was feeling. Continuing Jacob said

"For you to abdicate, him to replace you and...me by his side as co-regent."

"He wants you to rule with him? He doesn't ask for much does he?" She walked over to the table staring at the military map.

"Smart plan of his though, with you by his side makes sense. You would appease those that would stand against him on the council and in parliament. However, he's over playing his hand," continued the Queen.

Jacob walked over next to his mother and pointed to the MagiWolf army on the map.

"I wouldn't be so sure. That's not the only army he has. He told me he would have control over the barrier on the White Islands in a matter of hours and has allied with the American Republic on the other side...he gave me until the afternoon, three o clock for us to surrender to his terms."

The Queen smiled in admiration, "Very clever. His ties to the Americans has given him a ready made army and with nearly half of our forces pulled here to see off the MagiWolf he's divided us. Very clever indeed."

All of a sudden Jacob realised what his mother was alluding to and he panicked... "The Passing Arches! With the barrier down the American army will be able to pass straight into the Imperial City. Father?!"

The Queen shook her head in disagreement

"Not now the Passing Arch network has been shut down. During my visit to parliament before arriving here we agreed that the threat from Lady Regent Catherine was significant enough to temporarily suspend the network and send your father with a warship and forces to secure Farland Island. It'll only slow down the inevitable though. We've known for some time the Republic have been building ships, we didn't know their intentions for these ships before but now…now it seems clear—"

"They mean to sail their forces to attack the Imperial City," Jacob interrupted, finishing his mother's sentence as she nodded in reply.

"& I'd wager they are on their way, if not there already," the Queen continued.

"Shouldn't we return?!" Jacob said impatiently.

"Most of the Royal Council are in the City, along with our entire navy and the rest of the Royal Guard. They can defend themselves. Besides, we have a threat here to deal with and an opportunity to capture Thomas Colet and stop this before it turns into all out war."

"You think we can capture him?"

The Queen looked at Jacob with a subtle smile, *"We have over two thousand royal guards and you and I to lead them. You're one of the most gifted sorcerers in the world and while I maybe in my seventies now my power is ever strong. We go to war with Thomas Colet today, and we will win."*

Silence between them grew for a few moments as Jacob looked at his mother, studying her. After a few deep breaths Jacob nodded.

"I'll fight with you today. Because it's clear to me Thomas wishes a return to the ways of The Dark Knights rule but when we are done with this. With him. I don't know where that leaves us. I do know you have to answer for concealing what happened. Thomas is not the boy I knew. He is the man you and your father made him. Dark and twisted with revenge. Everything that is happening right now is a result of those actions."

Jacob's eye contact with his mother was broken by the pub door opening. Camila stepped inside holding the door ajar...

"My apologies for interrupting your majesty, but the MagiWolf army has been sighted to be on the move," said Camila.

"Already? Thomas said he'd give us until three o clock to answer his terms!" exclaimed Jacob.

The Queen adjusted her robes and began to make her way towards the door.

"It would seem he's growing impatient," said the Queen now standing in the door way to the street.

Camila bowed her head, *"Our forces are ready to march on your orders."*

"Then we march," said the Queen as she and Camila stepped out into the street leaving Jacob in the King's Crest, alone. He took a final glance at the map, placed the hood of his robes over his head and followed them to face Thomas.

CHAPTER ELEVEN

LAST WORDS OF DIPLOMACY

Dark clouds loomed over the highlands hiding the sun. With them a threat of rain and thunder followed the two thousand strong Royal Guard army lead by Queen Ellaryne,

Prince Jacob with Elliot by his side and Royal Lady Kerr. They marched out of Colghorn village through the forest that lead to a large open valley floor surrounded by slanted hills of exposed rock and grassy moss. The Queen held out her hand signalling the army to stop as they arrived atop a rolling hill leading to the valley floor. A tactical decision on The Queen's behalf to make sure they had the higher ground in front of an old ruined castle which lay at the foot of the largest hills a few miles in the distance. Jacob searched the lands in front of the castle for signs of Thomas' MagiWolf army but could see none.

He looked at his mother confused, *"I thought they had been spotted moving?"* asked Jacob. The Queen looked over at Camila who shrugged.

"Our scouts saw them leave the castle..." replied Camila.

"Over there!" Shouted Elliot, pointing at the valley floor to the west.

A huge shimmering dome of wavy light appeared about a mile away from them. The domed masking spell began to fall, revealing an ocean of at least a thousand MagiWolves and an equalled number of their sorcerer masters. At the very front two figures stood, Thomas and another, Jacob assumed but it was too far away to tell for sure.

The Queen and Jacob walked to the edge of the sloped hill to try and get a clearer view. Queen Ellaryne raised her hand, palm open to her eye line and focused on the air in front. In an instant a small perfect circle of telescopic glass appeared less than a meter round in front of her. Jacob moved to stand behind her to get a clearer view. Through the telescopic glass he could see Thomas still in his plain dark robes stroking a MagiWolf's huge and ugly head and now he recognised instantly the person standing to Thomas's left.

"That's Neville!" Jacob exclaimed.

"To prove his influence over the White Islands and the barrier no dou-" the Queen cut short her sentence as she noticed Thomas had disappeared from her view...

An ear piercing 'POP' came from behind Jacob and The Queen.   Multiple shouts of concern came from the The Royal Guard as Jacob and The Queen turned around in an instant to see Thomas standing there with his hairless MagiWolf, its teeth drawn and growling at them. Elliot rushed forwarded with his wielding spear hoisted towards Thomas and the beast.

Thomas bent down and patted the MagiWolf's head and looked round smiling at Elliot, *"Calm yourself man, they'll be plenty of time for that."*

Elliot looked at Jacob for assurance, who was nodding and signalling him to lower his spear. Thomas now straightened himself after calming the MagiWolf and looked at The Queen and Jacob.

"Welcome to the Highlands, Mr Colet," said the Queen calmly. Thomas chuckled quietly.

Thomas pointed to the royal guard army *"So...I assume this means that my offer has been turned down, your majesty?*

"If by offer you mean the attempt to turn my son against me and take my crown? Then yes... I'm afraid, that offer has been turned down. But it does not mean diplomacy is at an end. I have a new offer for you, Mr Colet."

Thomas folded his arms and looked squarely at the Queen.

"The great Ellaryne is making me an offer? This I have to hear."

The Queen moved a few steps closer to Thomas, entirely unfazed by the MagiWolf now glaring at her

"We shouldn't be victims of our ancestor's crimes. Indeed your ancestor King Colet was guilty for a great many as was my father of his crime. You are of royal blood and so I offer you this...a position on the Royal Council. As a Royal Lord, you can discuss and raise your concerns about the humans peacefully. There is no need for war. Jacob has told me you have allies in the American Republic? Maybe together we can build a friendship with them instead of being foes?"

Thomas peered around the Queen to look at Jacob.

"And this is what you want, Jacob? To be 'friends?"

Jacob walked forward to stand next to his mother. *"I don't want war, Thomas. Neither should you. And yes, maybe we can be friends again."*

Thomas walked over and looked down at his MagiWolf army. *"And what do I tell them? Those men and women whose lives have been uprooted countless times. Dragged from their homes because the Humans are constantly building more and more cities and factories closer to our little villages. Our masking spells, hundreds of years old that hid our villages are taken down and destroyed by our own kind because we must keep our people a secret? No! All you are offering is more of the same. You think a title that is rightfully mine anyway, can lure me from my destiny?"*

"Your destiny, as you call it, is to war with us, your own kind, and to what aim? To unite us against the humans in an ultimate war? Your destiny will lead us to extinction. Centuries ago our ancestors thought the same. They fought each other when our numbers were greater than they are today and that war lasted for generations and it nearly destroyed us all. Today humans have created weapons capable of enormous destruction far beyond our own capabilities. We live like we do, in the shadows away from them to avoid their hateful influences and diseases," said the Queen.

"Fear...this is all I hear from you. Queen Ellaryne of the British Empire of Magic! The most powerful magical kingdom in the world. You say I will lead us to extinction. I say you are already sleepwalking us there. Perhaps it was a childish hope of mine to think my friend could see his mother for who she really is but he stands with you side by side even after knowing the truth. It's clear you're all blind together. Yes, Ellaryne, there will be war and it will unite us."

Thomas reached down to touch his MagiWolf as he looked solely at Jacob. *"If we meet down there on that battle field it will not be as friends, Jacob."*

'POP!'

Thomas and the MagiWolf had disappeared leaving only a hint of grey mist behind.

Queen Ellaryne turned around and faced her army of Royal Guards. So polished was her golden armour down her arm the guards could see their reflections if they looked hard enough.

"None of you have faced this type of enemy before. Indeed no one living has done before yesterday. The MagiWolf are a vicious and powerful animal and will take your life without question. But like any living thing, they have their weaknesses. For the MagiWolf it is their master. Without their master they are just a wild animal without a purpose. Their transportation abilities can only work with a line of sight and can only go as far. Use your wielding spears to summon blocking spells, this will hinder that ability. Today we fight for the lives of the children and the people of Colghorn Village and your Empire. We fight to avenge the merciless attack of the innocent lives that were taken only yesterday." The Queen raised her arms and she was lifted into the air angelically thirty feet above her army.

"WILL YOU FIGHT?" she bellowed.

"FOR THE EMPIRE! WE FIGHT! WE FIGHT! WE FIGHT!" shouted the Royal Guard army thrusting their wielding spears to the sky. Jacob, Elliot and Camila also joining in with the chanting. The Queen slowly floated back down to the ground and turned looking down to the MagiWolf army, Jacob and Camila joining by her side.

"Camila, is your platoon waiting for you at the rear of that castle?" asked the Queen.

"Yes, your majesty" replied Camila.

"Good, go to them. Attack as soon as we have met his forces in the valley" Commanded the Queen as she looked at Jacob. *"Jacob, I want you to capture Neville, alive if you can. Taking him as prisoner may give us leverage over the White Islands. I will lead our forces in this battle myself."*

A loud and deep rumble of thunder came from the sky followed by torrential rain. The Queen threw her fist into the sky and commanded:

"ATTACK!"

The war had begun.

CHAPTER TWELVE

THE BATTLE FOR LOYALTY

The Royal Guard army charged through the rain and wind. Most of them on foot lead by Jacob but the Queen lead a smaller more powerful force of guards airborne into the sky using wind spells to keep them aloft. The MagiWolf army was charging to meet them at the centre of the valley floor with Neville leading them. The ground shook like an earthquake as soldiers feet and MagiWolf paws struck and dug into the earth beneath them. If it wasn't for the ancient masking spell covering the entire MagiFolk Highland region the sounds of rumbling and screams from the armies would have been heard and felt by Humans for miles around.

Neville and his army were getting closer and closer to meeting Jacob and his forces. Close enough for Jacob to see the hate and adrenaline coursing through his eyes. The rumbling noise of the armies grew louder and louder with MagiWolf howls muffled amongst them. With less than ten meters between the two armies Jacob summoned a fire spell to his hands and prepared to spit the fire towards Neville just as a huge cracking of thunder came from directly above them. The Queen overhead summoned huge bolts of deadly lightening and hurtled them downwards striking the front line of the MagiWolf army and their masters. The smell of singed flesh and hair punctured the air as the bolts of lightening kept coming, relentlessly sparking fires as they struck the ground causing the MagiWolf's to scatter from their masters in the confusion. Jacob saw the opportunity and ordered all his forces to continue the charge into the flames and attack the MagiWolf masters. Firing bright and white hot bolts from their spears the Royal Guard engaged the masters. The bolts striking their bodies and sending them hurtling mercilessly through the air. Jacob now drawing on his own magic began to cast a fogging spell his eyes turning white as the magic coursed through his body casting the spell. A thick white fog appeared just behind the front line of the MagiWolf army. The master's began sending fire spells in random directions as the fog obscured their vision.

"JACOB!"

Elliot screamed as Jacob turned around a MagiWolf had leapt at him too late for him to cast a spell in defence. Its teeth drawn and inches from Jacob's throat but Elliot's spear was flying through the air striking the MagiWolf's ribs piercing its heart, dead as it struck the ground. Jacob relieved took a few steps back to regain his balance. Elliot ran over to him pulling his spear from the MagiWolf's lifeless body.

"You know, if you're going to cast a complicated spell like that fogging spell, you might want someone to watch your back while you do it!?" joked Elliot as the fighting continued around them.

"You were there weren't you?!" laughed Jacob, *"Right, time to find Neville."*

"Lady Kerr has engaged her forces from behind and the Queen has attacked the centre with Thomas no where to be seen. Looks like we are winning," said Elliot as the two searched for signs of Neville since Jacob lost sight of him during the lightening strikes. Suddenly Jacob saw him appearing from the white fog walking towards him, flanked by two masters and their MagiWolfs within the chaos of the fighting. Elliot had also now spotted him and stood next to Jacob his spear still dripping from the blood of the MagiWolf.

"Remember, the Queen wants him for a prisoner...that means alive, Jacob," said Elliot with Jacob simply nodding in reply as they came face to face.

"Looks like we are going to fight after all, Jacob! Pity my King has asked for you to be taken alive!" snarled Neville.

"Indeed! My Queen has ask the same of me for you," replied Jacob summoning magic to his hands sparking electricity bouncing from finger to finger.

"Think you can take care of the masters while I knock him out?" Jacob asked Elliot who smiled back

"Mmm, I've been wanting to show off my new air spell," replied Elliot.

Without another moment's hesitation Jacob sent a bolt of electricity from his hands at Neville who had summoned a barrier spell in response. The bolt crashed into the barrier with a crack disarming the spell completely. Jacob adapted and cast a second spell of water spiralling down from the sky directly above Neville engulfing him in drowning water. Jacob then re-summoned his electricity spell firing another bolt into the spiralling mass of water trapping Neville. The bolt hit the water and conducted through it into Neville shocking him enough to render him unconscious. Meanwhile, Elliot planted his spear into the ground and stood in a lunging stance summoning the air spell with his arms raised to the sky. A wind began to pick up quickly around him and the masters who had commanded their MagiWolf's to attack him. In an instant the wind spell had whipped around the masters like an invisible rope. They gasped for air but no air came as their lungs were being crushed and as they fell to the ground suffocating the MagiWolfs fled into the fog confused as their masters were defeated.

Both the masters and Neville lay motionless on the ground as the noise from the armies had grown quiet and no howls could be heard from the MagiWolfs. Jacob and Elliot stood side by side looking at them as Jacob began to clear the fog. As the fog dispelled they could see hundreds of lifeless bodies on the ground. The dead masters and MagiWolfs outnumbering the Royal guards dead ten to one.

"Looks like we won then?" said Elliot looking at the killing fields.

"Looks like?" replied Jacob.

From behind the Queen walked towards them with a hundred of the guards behind her.

"Thomas fled. Seems he had some kind of Passing Arch we didn't know about. Took what forces he had with him," said the Queen.

"I did what you asked," said Jacob pointing at Neville's unconscious body laying on the ground.

"Excellent, my son, and you Elliot... Guards take Neville back to the village and secure him there," said the Queen.

"What now?" asked Jacob of his mother.

"Now we go home and find out what Thomas's next move will be," responded the Queen as she looked back at the surviving Royal Guards.

Jacob looked around at his surroundings and back at his mother, *"And how are we getting home with the Passing Arch network down?"*

"There's an Imperial ship waiting for us off the coast just west of here. We will take what guards that can summon air spells and fly with us there. The ship will take us back to the

Imperial City. Hopefully we will get there before any of Thomas's forces from the American Republic."

CHAPTER THIRTEEN

THE VOYAGE HOME

Jacob embraced the fresh highland air hitting his face as he flew through the now clearing sky. The Queen, Elliot and Lady Camila leading a handful of Royal Guards behind them towards the west coast. The sun hung low on the horizon as the darkness of night came. Jacob looked to his side to see his mother with the air flowing through her hair. She felt his eyes resting on her and looked at him. Like the air that was between them as they flew, Jacob felt a growing feeling of uncertainty and mistrust for her. This troubled him greatly as he would never have believed he could feel anything else other than love and admiration for her and he honestly didn't know how they'd fix this void between them or even if they could at all. His thoughts were broken as he saw her pointing to something in the distance. He narrowed his eyes to see a large ship a few miles out to sea. Lead by the Queen they all began to descend closer to the ship. A large war ship style vessel, its sharp and sleek silver lines glistening in the last of the sunset light. Twenty or so men and women stood on the forward deck between two large gun turrets to welcome the Queen and her company as they touched down on the ship's deck.

The Queen and Jacob set down first, landing softly on the deck with Camila, Elliot and the guards behind them. A clean shaven man dressed in an all white naval jacket and trousers with silver studded buttons up to his neck stepped forward and bowed to the Queen. His medals along his left shoulder hanging down and clunking as he lowered.

"Your majesty. I am Captain Elijah Osbond. Welcome aboard the B.E.M. Sabre."

"Thank you, Captain. We are to sail at your best speed to the Imperial city at once."

The Captain motioned the Queen to walk with him below deck. She looked back at Jacob to beckon him with them as she pointed to the guards & continuing said,

"These brave men and women of the Royal Guard are tired and hungry, Captain. See to it they are fed and rested tonight please."

Jacob, Elliot and Camila followed the Queen and the Captain below deck. The corridors were decked with dark wood and grey concrete floors. Small circular portholes with candle lit lanterns on either side looking out at the ocean.

"Of course your Majesty. We have prepared state rooms for you, the Prince and Royal Lady Kerr as well," replied the

Captain as he showed the Queen to her stateroom door. She turned round to look at Jacob and Camila.

"I'd like the two of you to join me later. We have much to discuss. Eat and rest a while first," said the Queen. Jacob nodded as he realised just how tired and hungry he was. There was something about the serenity of being on the ocean that made him relax for the first time in many days. The Captain showed Jacob to his stateroom opposite his mothers. Thanking the Captain Jacob then opened the door to let Elliot enter first, the Captain looked confused, *"He's with me, Captain."* The Captain nodded quickly, *"Of course your highness."* Jacob followed Elliot into the room and closed the dark wooden door behind him.

The room was simple enough, a small double bed with a wooden chair and desk at one side and a lantern lit porthole on the other. Elliot sat down on the bed removing his armour and placing his spear beside the chair. He looked up into Jacob's eyes which began to fill with tears. Elliot leapt from the bed and held him as tightly as he could. Jacob began to weep softly on his shoulder.

"Everything...everyone I believed in...it's a lie Elliot. It's all a lie!" sobbed Jacob. Elliot lent forward and looked into Jacob's eyes brushing away the tears with his hands.

"What are you talking about? What lie?"

"Thomas's family wasn't murdered by random extremists. It was the King. My grandfather. He killed them...because...because he was a Colet. My mother and the

Royal Council covered it up. And she...killed him...the King." The tears were streaming faster and faster from Jacob's bloodshot eyes.

"She?"

"My mother!" Jacob cried softly. They both laid back on the bed holding each other staring up at the wooden ceiling.

"In her defence, I suppose she was only doing what she felt was right?" said Elliot. Jacob looked at him with a hint of anger.

"You agree with her?" asked Jacob, surprised. Elliot shook his head and frowned in thought.

"It's not that I agree with her, it's more about...what would you have done different? I mean...the idea that our King was a killer of a seemingly innocent family...I can't imagine what that would have done to our people. There would have been riots in the streets. Maybe even a civil war. By covering it up, she made sure that didn't happen and if she did kill him for it, that would have been some justice, wouldn't it?"

They both stared at each other for while, Jacob studying his words.

"Whether she was right or not, even if she did avert all of that...what's happening now is a direct result of those actions. It's turned the boy I grew up with, that was bright and funny into a dark and vengeful man. But the most painful thing about it all is that, I am so full of anger for what she did I don't know *if I can ever forgive her,"* said Jacob looking back up at the ceiling. A single tear falling from his eye. Elliot still looking at him and holding him close.

"Are you angry for what she did or because she kept it from you?" asked Elliot.

Jacob frowned hard and shrugged *"Huh?…what's the difference?"*

"The difference is, mistakes can be forgiven but a trust broken…I think that's much harder to forgive."

Jacob rolled over to one side with Elliot putting his arm around him. They closed their eyes and almost as quickly they fell asleep.

BANG BANG BANG

Jacob and Elliot woke with a huge start. Elliot got to his feet instantly, putting himself between Jacob and the room door.

"Your highness? The Queen has requested your presence in her stateroom!" bellowed a man's voice from the other side of their door.

"Blimey man, you trying to give us a heart attack in here?" shouted back Elliot through the door.

"Yes yes, fine. I'll be along in a moment," Jacob replied to the man.

"How long were we asleep?" said Jacob rubbing his eyes as he sat up from the bed, stretching out his back from right to left.

"Not long I don't think. You better go to her," said Elliot. Jacob got up from the bed and walked over to the door while straightening his robes. He opened the door and motioned to walk out, but Elliot quickly grabbed his shoulder and pulled him around to kiss him. They smiled at each other.

"She loves you, Jacob. Remember, you're her one true prince!" Elliot flamboyantly threw his hands in the air and they both laughed.

"You idiot. I love you, you know," said Jacob earnestly.

"Oh I know it." Elliot closed the door as Jacob crossed the deck to his mother's stateroom. He knocked softly and breathed in deeply. The door was opened by a royal guard and Jacob walked into a much bigger version of his stateroom with a large open lounge with two sofas. Camila had already arrived sitting in the corner of the room next to a round table. The Queen stood staring out of the porthole into the night. She moved her head to the side slightly catching the guard's eye, "Thank you, you may leave us now please." The guard did as the Queen commanded and left the room closing the door firmly behind him.

Jacob took the free seat on the other side of the table where Camila was sat. He looked at her and nodded.

"My apologies if I'm late. I fell asleep," said Jacob.

The Queen turned round to face them both smiling warmly. *"No doubt you did. It's been a long few days."*

"So...? What are we here to talk about, mother?" asked Jacob impatiently.

"I spoke with the Captain. As he sailed up to meet with us he spotted five or more ships heading for the Imperial City.. He believed they were from the American Republic and each big enough to carry at least two hundred soldiers. If this information is correct it means that my husband the Prince Maybook and his forces we sent to secure the White Islands have been thwarted."

Jacob opened his mouth to speak but the Queen stopped him.

"We do not know your father's fate, Jacob. He is valuable and I would expect him to be taken prisoner. Either way, this means the barrier has fallen and by the time we reach the Imperial City they will have already began their attack. The reality is stark. The battle at Colghorn meant we committed almost half of our entire forces, most of which are stranded there until we can reopen the Passing Arch network. With our forces divided we do not have the numbers to defend the Imperial City. This was a deliberate move by Thomas. Forcing us to engage him there while his American allies sailed. I have no doubt Thomas Colet will be leading this attack himself. To ensure the city falls to him.

Therefore, I see we only have one option and it is NOT to surrender... With the small force of guards we have onboard this ship I will lead an attack on Thomas himself!"

Jacob stood up to interrupt his mother. *"No way! Not only is he very powerful, he will undoubtedly be protected by his best people! Even if you took every guard here, he'd see you coming...he'll be expecting it!"*

"Yes! Precisely! The attack is a distraction. No matter what is going on in that city, when I am spotted he'll throw everything he has at me. He knows I'm powerful, he knows that's the only way he can defeat me."

"And what is this distraction for, your majesty?" asked Camila.

"While I have the attention of Thomas and his allied forces, you, Jacob and Elliot will make your way to the Passing Dome. Jacob and Elliot will open an arch to our forces in Colghorn while you, Camila, will use this to open an arch to the French Kingdom." The Queen held out a small glass key and gave it to Camila.

"The Passing Arch this activates will take you directly to King Jean's private villa in southern France. He is an old friend and ally of mine. You will ask him for his help. Explain how we got here, he knew my father well...and I hope he'll understand, at least enough to help us. If Thomas gets what he wants, a war with the humans will engulf us all."

Looking at his mother, Jacob still didn't know how to feel about her and the actions she was taking.

"Camila, I now need to speak with my son, privately." Camila stood up from her chair and walked up to the Queen and took her hand in hers.

"You are the bravest person I've ever known, your majesty." Camila looked back at Jacob with her eyes glassing over. She walked to the door and left the room. The Queen sat down in the now vacant seat by Jacob and took his hand that had been resting on the table but Jacob pulled his away from her touch. In that moment Jacob could almost hear his mothers heart break but there was still too much anger and confusion in him. She looked up into his eyes.

"Jacob, this is important. Tomorrow, one way or another, your world is going to change dramatically. No matter what happens, you must know everything that I've done has been for you and my people. I love you with everything I have. One day, this Empire will be yours to rule. To govern how you see fit. Lead with your heart, Jacob. That will sometimes mean you make mistakes, but they will be mistakes you can live with."

Jacob stared down at his mothers open hand still reaching out on the table for his. He desperately wanted to take her hand and somehow knew he'd regret it if he didn't but couldn't. He wouldn't. Instead he stood up from the table his expression blank.

"*Is that all then?*" As he spoke the words his voice began to break and chin tensed with emotion.

His mother stood up to meet him and smiled while looking right into his eyes.
"*Just one more thing...keep Elliot close. He loves you above all else and he is truly loyal. He'll guide you well when the time comes.*"

Jacob nodded and reached for the door handle.

"*I'll see you in the morning,*" he walked out and closed the door of the stateroom leaving the Queen alone.

He stood there in the corridor for what felt like an eternity. The urge to go back in and hug his mother was taking control of him and just as he motioned to go back to her, the ship's porter carrying a tray full of plates with food walked into the corridor. Jacob pulled back away from the Queen stateroom door.

"*Excuse me, your highness?*"

"*Ye...YES?*" Jacob stuttered and cleared his throat.

"*Dinner for you and your partner, sire. Would you like me to take it into your stateroom?*"

"*Oh, thank you, yes.*" Jacob pointed his hand towards his stateroom door.

The porter knocked and opened the door taking the tray of food and resting it down on the small table in front of the bed where Elliot was sat cleaning the MagiWolf blood off his spear. Jacob motioned for the porter to leave who made his way out of the stateroom at once.

"Oh before you go, what time tomorrow are we expected to arrive at the Imperial City?" asked Jacob as the porter was on the threshold of their doorway.

"Soon after mid-morning I believe, your highness," replied the porter. Jacob smiled in thanks at the porter and closed the door. He and Elliot sat down at the small wooden table and began lifting the silver coverings over the plates to reveal steaming hot steaks and two glasses of red wine on the side.

"They live alright on these ships don't they!" chuckled Elliot.

Jacob smiled forcefully. Elliot could see he was upset, perhaps even more so than he was earlier.

"How did the meeting with your mother go?" asked Elliot as they both tucked into the food.
"She's going to fight Thomas while we get to the Passing Dome" said Jacob as they both took sips of wine. *"And she gave me some leadership advice."*

"Good advice was it?"

Jacob looked at Elliot warmly and smiled more genuinely

"To keep you close by."

Elliot picked up his glass of wine and held it out to cheers Jacob'

"Blimey, that's advice I can drink too!" Jacob laughed and clinked his glass with Jacob. The two continued eating whilst Jacob explained in more detail the plan his mother had set out. They savoured this moment of time together as neither knew when they'd get a moment like this again after they reached the Imperial City and the fighting started.

CHAPTER FOURTEEN

THE NEW DARK DAWN

Jacob began to wake. The rocking of the ship lulling him gently. In these blissful few moments the memories of the last forty eight hours had not reached his conscious mind. Instead he felt at ease and comfortable in the sublime ignorance. Sunlight began to beam into the room resting warmly on his face. He turned instinctively in the bed reaching out for Elliot but felt only an empty cold space. He opened his blurry eyes, rubbing them softly.

"Elliot?" Jacob eyes searched the room for him and then noticed a small piece of paper on Elliot's bedside pillow.

" Morning sleepy! Your mother has asked for me. Thought I'd let you sleep in. We'll be waiting on the bridge for you. Love you. E. Xxx

Jacob laughed to himself as he could see Elliot's expressions as he wrote the note in his mind. He then looked over and noticed a fresh set of plain dark robes that had been left folded at the end of the bed with a note and his name written on it. He got up and tried them on. Clearly this is what his mother wanted him to wear to aid an incognito approach to the Passing Dome.

"These are the plainest and dullest thing I've ever worn. Thank you mother!" he said aloud to himself with a slight chuckle in his voice.

He cleaned himself up and made his way out of the stateroom and down the deck trying to find his way to the bridge. He couldn't remember much about the ship's layout when they arrived due to the fact he was so tired and hungry. One of the ships crewmen came down a small brass spiral staircase to the left of the deck. The crewman was slightly startled when he recognised Jacob as the Prince in such normal and plain clothes. He stopped and bowed to Jacob much lower than was necessary, clearly flustered and red in the face.

"Your highness!" said the young crewman.

"Good morning crewmen. Could you tell me which way It is to the bridge, please?" The crewman was surprised and taken back by Jacob's politeness that he stumbled his words *"Errh, yes Prince, I mean, your highness. It's up these stairs and on the portside, that's to the left...you'll see a large bulkhead...a door sire."*

Jacob nodded and smiled and was now waiting for the crewman to move as he blocked his way. Jacob raised his eyebrows as the crewman realised he was in his way.

"Oh, sorry!" said the crewman.

He scuttled off as Jacob laughed and made his way up the small cramped brass staircase. As he reached the top he saw the large mettle bulkhead to the left as the crewman said it would be. The door was guarded by two royal guards with their wielding spears. The guards bowed to Jacob and opened the bulkhead to the bridge. Jacob walked inside into a long deck of crewman sitting at their stations and the Captain sat in his chair in the middle overlooking the front of the ship. Elliot, Camila and his mother were gathered to the right looking down studying a large map chart. They looked up as they noticed Jacob had entered. Elliot smiled and winked at him while his mother beckoned with her hand for him to join them.

"I take it you slept well, my son?" asked the Queen kindly

"Apologies, I appear to have slept in a little too late," Jacob said looking over at Elliot accusingly, "where are we?"

"We'll be coming up on the Imperial City very soon, your highness!" answered Captain Osbond.

"As you can see we've been hugging the coastline for the entire approach to the Imperial City. Thanks to this vessel's masking spell we've been hidden from Human and MagiFolk's eyes alike, giving us a slight advantage." said the Queen as she pointed down to the map chart. Jacob could see the outline of the island where the Imperial City and Royal Palace rested. The Queen continued,

"We sent one scout from the royal guard early this morning to see if the attack had begun."

"And?" asked Jacob.

"He has not returned. Which means the attack has most likely begun and they know we are coming," replied Camila. Jacob looked at each of them for their reactions.

"We must brace ourselves with what we may find when we come around that headland and see the City."

The Queen pointed towards the glass windows at the front of the bridge to a large coastal line of headlands with rocks that rolled into the sea and waves crashing upon them. Jacob looked out, he now noticed that the sky was glowing a reddish colour passed the headlands. At first he thought it was the sunrise but he realised it was too late in the morning for that. He frowned and walked over to the Captain,

"Captain, what is that?" asked Jacob pointing to the reddened horizon.

"We believe it to be caused by fire, your highness..." answered the Captain.

"The city? How much fire would there need to be to cause that much light pollution?"

The Captain looked out to the horizon with Jacob. *"A lot, sire...a lot,"* he said with sorrow in his voice as he stood up and walked to the other side of the room where he pulled a large gramophone style horn close to his mouth.

"All hands. We are turning into Regents Bay. The Imperial City is under attack. Prepare all stations for battle!" bellowed the Captain.

"Jacob! Come here. The time has come," the Queen called him back to the map chart. *"I will take the royal guard with me airborne and draw out Thomas, meanwhile the Captain will attack the American ships to distract them. The three of you are to take that opportunity to fly low and into the palace courtyard and make your way to the Passing Dome. We have no idea how far Thomas' forces have penetrated the city or if they have reached the palace itself but you know the city better than them and you're more powerful. The guard is waiting for me at the front of the ship...I must join them now."* She looked at Jacob longingly and without warning hugged him so tightly

his ribs hurt. His arms locked down by his side he just stood rigid. She pulled back and nodded at him and turned to Camila and Elliot.

"Keep each other safe."

The Queen walked outside leaving the bridge through the bulkhead to meet the Royal Guard. Jacob walked over to the bridge windows overlooking the front of the ship to see his mother join them. Her golden armour this time surrounded her entire torso and neck. A long white cape hung down trailing along the floor of the ship's deck. Less than twenty of the remaining guards stood in a perfect square to her command. With a huge cheer of royal motivation they held their spears to the sky as the Queen launched rapidly into the air high above them and the ship. The royal guards followed close behind collectively launching into the sky. The ship then began to turn around the point of the headlands and into Regents Bay.

The first thing Jacob saw was the flames. They roared so high and fiercely out of the City that it looked like the ocean was on fire itself. Six ships encircled the Island all relentlessly firing cannons of fiery balls into the city. The statues of the past Kings and Queens were also struck and crumbling into the ocean below. Jacob saw his mother and the royal guard to the east of the city attacking a small group of Thomas' masters who were also airborne, using air spells to fly. Bolts of blue lightning shot from the Queen's forces into the masters causing them to fall lifeless out of the sky.

"She's making quick work of Colet's masters!" said Elliot.

"*They don't stand a chance against her.*" Jacob replied matter of factly. He once again began to feel the pride for his mother as she flew fearlessly into battle.

"*As soon as Colet shows himself we will engage the American fleet. That's also your cue to get to the Passing Dome, your highness,*" said the Captain.

"*Where is our fleet?*" asked Camila.

"*To the west my lady. Or what's left of it.*" The Captain pointed to three ships burning and sinking. Jacob summoned the telescopic glass spell to see hundreds of the ships crew jumping off the decks into the water.

"*They're going to drown! We have to help them!*" Jacob demanded.

"*We can't, your highness! As soon as we enter the city's masking spell it will render ours useless and we will be attacked! We have to wait*" replied the Captain.

"*Look!*" exclaimed Elliot. He pointed to where the Queen and her guard forces, but heading towards them were a greater force of masters with wings of fire on either side coming from a figure in front. It was an incredible display of magical power and could only mean one thing.

"*That has to be Thomas!*" said Jacob. They all agreed and they knew what that meant. It was time for Jacob, Camila and Elliot to leave.

"Helm. Full ahead for the city. Breach the masking spell walls and fire everything we have at the flag ship in the middle!" yelled the Captain. He looked over and Jacob and bowed,*"Time to leave, your highness!"*

"Good luck, Captain!" said Jacob as he left for the bulkhead and headed to the outside deck, Elliot and Camila following closely behind they too in plain dark robes identical to Jacob's. The salty air hit their faces as they stepped outside and looked out to the city.

Jacob turned to the both of them,*"We know what we have to do! Masking spells won't work once we are within the city's magic wards and its own masking spell barrier. So we fly low and fast. Stay close to me and don't do anything to draw attention so us."* Jacob instinctively took command, this was what he was born for.

The three stood together and summoned their air spells. With a gust of cold wind the three of them launched quickly into the air their robes flapping behind them. At high speed they swooped together quickly over the ship's decks and down just a few feet above the ocean. Jacob looked up to where his mother had now engaged with Thomas himself. Multiple cracks of the most powerful lightening spells that Jacob had ever seen came from the Queen crashing into Thomas's barrier defence spells sending huge shockwaves of sound and light through the sky. Elliot flew up closer to Jacob who was also watching the epic battle between the two above them.

"I'VE NEVER SEEN SPELLS THAT POWERFUL BEFORE!" shouted Elliot as Jacob struggled to hear him over the wind just as three fiery cannon balls came whooshing a few feet above them fired by the Sabres gun turrets impacting the American flag ship squarely in the middle of their hull and causing catastrophic damage.

"LOOKS LIKE THE CAPTAIN IS OUT FOR BLOOD!"

Shouted Elliot again. Jacob spotted a section of the City's walls that had been breached at the rear of the island, he pointed it out to both Elliot and Camila but it was being blocked by two of the sinking flagships flanking vessels.

"OVER THERE! WE CAN SNEAK UP THE BACK AND AROUND TO THE FRONT OF THE PALACE. STAY LOW!"

Shouted Jacob as the two of them gave a thumbs up to confirm they'd heard him. They flew round to the side of the American flag ship with its crew members now jumping overboard to flee the flames. The two flanking ships had now moved to join together and began their return assault on the Sabre. As Jacob twisted his head back he could see the Sabre being pounded relentlessly by the return fire. Although it was hard for him to witness it meant that the American ships were distracted enough for them to enter the rear of the city unnoticed.

They flew as low and close to each other as they could towards the rear of the city where the cannon fire from the enemy ships had breached the wall creating a hole big enough for them to fly through.

"SINGLE FILE THROUGH THE WALL!"

Jacob shouted as Camila and Elliot fell into line right behind him. As they passed through the wall they flew closely over the streets of the outer city. Jacob looked down and could see hoards of people running and fleeing their homes as the masters casted fire spells at them and their MagiWolfs charged into the innocent fleeing crowds. All three of them desperately wanted to land down there and help defend the people but they knew they couldn't. They had to get to the Passing Dome while Thomas and his navy were distracted.

The three weaved in and out of the city's stone buildings and thick black smoke that was now covering most of the city making sure they were not spotted as they drew closer to the palace. Finally as they began to climb higher with the city's elevation they reached the Palace outer wall but Jacob saw what he feared...the palace gate had been smashed down. The masters were inside the palace grounds. He searched for an area for them to set down unnoticed. Although the gates were breached he couldn't see any masters or Royal Guards within the grounds. He signalled them to descend into the gardens below them. Jacob headed for the large tree at the edge of the gardens, the very tree he used to climb when he was a child. Camila and Elliot followed him down and then landed softly underneath the tree. Jacob patted his hand in a downward motion signalling them to crouch down behind the tree. The three of them looked around eagle eyed assessing their surroundings. The once beautifully manicured gardens was now a wasteland to fallen rubble, ash and burning embers charring the grass. A huge **boom** and **crack** shook the ground they stood on. The three peered through the branches of the trees to catch only glimpses of the enduring battle of magic between Thomas and the Queen. Jacob couldn't see clearly, just blinding flashes of blue and orange. Camila tugged at Jacob's robes to get his attention.

"Through there!" whispered Camila as she motioned towards a stone path behind them that was covered by burning trees on either side. *"It leads to the courtyard,* Jacob nodded slowly.

"Okay...alright, let's do this. Stay right behind me. Don't stop for anything or anyone. Okay?" said Jacob and the two nodded in agreement as they huddled as close to each other without stepping on the other's feet.

"Go!" Jacob set off running towards the stone path with Elliot and Camila sprinting close behind. They rushed along the pathway dodging and jumping over the fallen branches flaming with fire and the singeing embers burning their robes as they ran. The path finally opened up into the royal courtyard with the ivy covered alleyway to the left that lead straight to the Passing Dome. Jacob stopped them behind a blackened burnt out tree just at the corner of the courtyard. Two masters and their MagiWolfs were patrolling the alleyway entrance. Jacob looked back at Elliot and Camila knowing what he had to do.

"You two stay hidden here, I'll take care of them!" Elliot pulled Jacob's shoulder back as he motioned forward.

"No! I'm the one that's meant to protect you! I'll go," protested Elliot as he stood up, but Jacob placed his hands on his shoulders pushing him back down.

"That may well be, but I'm a lot more powerful! Keep an eye out on the other side of the courtyard," ordered Jacob as he stood back up, placed his hood over his head and walked out into the courtyard in full view of the masters. As they spotted him their MagiWolfs tensed their hairless bodies and drew their teeth growling at him. Jacob stood in front of them and lowered his hood. The masters looked at each other as they recognised who he was.

Jacob then lowered his hands down by his side, palms open.

"I can't say I appreciate what you've done to my mother's garden, gentlemen!". Both masters summoned fire spells to their hands but Jacob threw his arms forward slamming his palms together with a huge crack piercing the air and cast a pushing spell that sent a shockwave so powerful through the air that the ground lifted between them shattering every bone in the bodies of the masters and MagiWolfs as the shockwave passed through them sending their broken bodies flying backwards through the air landing twenty feet away. He looked back at Elliot and Camila and waved them to come out. They ran over to Jacob and followed him down the ivy alleyway towards the Passing Dome.

Elliot ran up to Jacob's side, "Remind me never to piss you off!" exclaimed Elliot with Jacob smiling as they reached the last corner of the alleyway. Jacob stopped and peered round to make sure the way was clear.

"Alright, I can see the Dome. Our guards are there...but looks like they're dead. No masters or MagiWolfs either, the way is clear, let's go!" . The three walked cautiously up the Passing Dome entrance looking in every direction for signs of a master or MagiWolf but all was quiet.

"There must be more masters around here? Where are they?" asked Elliot.

"I would assume they've gone up to the higher palace to capture the Royal Council members," answered Camila as she looked up at the towering stone palace to their right.

"Camila's right. And the sooner we can get the rest of our forces from Colghorn the better," said Jacob.
"Talking of which, what is the plan once we've brought them here?" asked Elliot as they opened the large glass door to the Dome.

"You and I will take a small force to the higher palace and secure the Royal Council. Meanwhile, we need the rest of the guards to form a ring around the outer palace walls in order to create a new barrier spell around the entire palace," said Jacob as they took a few steps inside the now darkened and eerie Dome. All the arches were absent of the magical shimmering light, just a dark empty space remained in its place.

"There hasn't been a barrier spell cast that big in centuries, Jacob," whispered Camila in Jacob's ear.

"Which is why we need the Royal Council to help me cast it. Together with the royal guards using their wielding spears dug into the earth along the outer palace walls it should be enough power to create a barrier spell between us and the rest of Thomas' forces. Elliot, you'll need to take what's left of the guard and help evacuate the survivors of the city behind the palace walls."

The three of them now stood in the centre of the Dome as he pointed to the largest of the Passing Arches in front of them.

"That's the one we used to get to Colghorn a few days ago. We just need to figure out how to turn the bloody thing on...any ideas?" asked Jacob as he looked round at the two of them who were staring back at him blankly.

"Brilliant!" said Jacob defeatedly, but then they heard the sound of shuffled foot steps coming from the far corner of the Dome. Elliot instantly summoned a fire spell into his palm ready to attack at an instant but the flickering fire from his spell through a dim light over a small figure emerging from the darkness.

"Your highness? Oh it is you!" the old caretaker lady threw herself into Jacob's arms and embraced him.

"Your the caretaker, aren't you?" said Jacob as she took a few steps back from him and looked up at his face, her eyes filling with tears of relief.

"Yes. I've been hidden here since the palace wall was breached. I...I thought they would come for the Passing Dome but they went straight into the palace, there were too many for our guards to stop them. The Queen!? Is she—"

"——She's here leading the assault, but she needs us to open the large arch to Colghorn to bring back our forces that are stranded there. Can you help us?" asked Jacob. The caretaker pushed back her shoulders and composed herself quickly.

"Of course! As the Queen commands! This way!" Grabbing Jacob's arm she lead them towards the large arch in a few meters in front of them.

"How do we turn it on?" asked Elliot and the caretaker looked at them with a cunning smile. She walked up to the side of the stone archway and placed her hand softly on the stone.

"The responsibility of the caretaker has been handed down through my family for generations. We alone have been entrusted with the ability to control the arches in this Dome."

A soft warming reddish light emitted from the old lady's palm as she touched the arch. All of a sudden the shimmering light filled the Passing Arch giving off a cold breeze. The three of them stood back marvelling at it. Camila walked over to the caretaker and pulled out the glass key that the Queen had given her. The caretaker looked down at the key and nodded knowingly.

"The Queen has asked me to go on a separate errand to the French Kingdom. Do you know which arch the key belongs to?" asked Camila as Jacob and Elliot watched on.

"Of course, this is the Queen's key. This way."

The caretaker walked back into the darkness of the Dome motioning for Camila to come with her. Camila took both Jacob and Elliot's hands, *"Good luck you two. I'll be seeing you soon with the king's help I hope,"*

"Take the caretaker with you. It's too dangerous for her here and you might need her on the other side," said Jacob and the three of them said their farewells for now. Jacob and Elliot turned back to the Colghorn archway.

"Right then, let's go get us an army!" said Jacob as the two of them disappeared through the arch.

CHAPTER FIFTEEN

THE FALL

"TO YOUR FEET!" Jacob commanded. Fifteen hundred Royal Guards instantly leaped to their feet, their spears in their hands as they saw Jacob and Elliot standing at the threshold of a newly appeared huge archway of shimmering light behind.

"YOUR QUEEN HAS ORDERED YOU TO FIGHT! THE IMPERIAL CITY IS FALLING AND YOUR QUEEN FIGHTS AS WE SPEAK. TAKE YOUR ORDERS FROM COMMANDER ELLIOT AS YOU FOLLOW ME THROUGH THE ARCH TO THE CITY TO DEFEND THE PALACE!"

Elliot walked down the village square where the guards had gathered and began forming them into groups as they marched as one into the passing arch crossing back into the the Dome lead by Jacob. Quickly, the Passing Dome filled with guards ready for battle. Every inch of the ground inside the Dome was now occupied by the royal guard. Jacob and Elliot stood at the large glass Dome entrance ready.

"They have their orders?" Jacob asked Elliot.

"They do! I've also got ten of them to come with us to the higher palace," before Jacob could reply the entire Dome shook with a loud rumble and flash of lightening causing debris to fall from the ceiling making the two wince with worry.

"Sounds like your mother is still giving Thomas a beating!" said Elliot.

"But she won't be able to keep it up for long. We have to hurry."

The concern in his voice for his mother was obvious, *"Let's go!"* said Jacob. Elliot and Jacob threw open the glass doors of the Passing Dome and charged out back through the wide ivy covered alleyway leading back into the palace court yard. The ground was shaking with the pounding feet of the Royal Guard that followed behind them. As they ran into the large open court yard the guard broke off into their separate divisions. Some headed out into the city to evacuate the people and the rest began forming the ring around the outer palace walls stabbing their spears into the ground ready for the barrier spell to be cast. Jacob, Elliot and ten other guards headed towards the palace entrance. The huge stone and steel door had been smashed down and lay broken in pieces in front of them. Jacob then looked up to find his mother who was still fighting Thomas. Bolts of blue light coming from both of them meeting in the middle. The two were in the midst of a magical power struggle with Thomas looking like he's gaining power over his mother. Jacob had to get the barrier spell up now. His mother didn't have long.

"It'll take too long going through the palace stairs. We have to fly up!" commanded Jacob. The guards all looked anxiously at each other.

"Sire! We can't cast air spells powerful enough to fly!" said the guard closest to Jacob.

"You let us worry about that. Gather round me closely." Jacob looked at Elliot and they lowered their heads focusing

their minds to cast an air spell big and powerful to lift them all up. Sure enough together they lifted swiftly into the air and climbed quickly up the palace wall towards the higher palace.

They slowed their ascent as they reached Jacob's apartment balcony.

"We'll enter through my apartment, the Royal Council's chamber near enough."

They floated onto the balcony stone floor softly and into Jacob's living room. Everything was as he left it only a few days before. To Jacob it felt like a lifetime ago he was here.

"Quickly!" Jacob motioned the guards and Elliot out into the large palace hall that lead directly to the Royal Council chamber. They could hear yelling and screaming from behind the chamber doors. They quickly, but silently made their way to the doors as Jacob as quietly as he could opened the big stone doors to peer inside the chamber room just enough to see with one eye. Flashes of light and fire is all he could make out and then he saw one of the Royal Lords being held against the floor by a master and his MagiWolf.

"They're in there! Okay. We go in and take out the masters first then the MagiWolfs." Everyone agreed with Jacob's plan as they took a few steps back. Jacob cupped both his hands together and summoned another pushing spell to blast open the doors. He threw the spell at the doors and they smashed open sending sharp pieces of stone debris towards the masters who turned round in complete shock and surprise

trying to recover from the explosion. The Royal Council members were huddled together behind the upturned stone High Table. Elliot and the guards fired pushing spells and fire spells at the masters. Some of them blocking with barrier spells but most of them being struck hard backwards onto the floor. The guards then attacked the MagiWolfs with their spears. Two masters circled Jacob who had cut him off from Elliot and the guards. They fired their fire spells at Jacob who summoned a barrier spell and blocked them. He then cast an air spell and lifted the two masters crashing into the ceiling and then throwing them down to the stone floor with a crack.

"That's all of them!" said Elliot.

The nine Royal Ladies and Lords of the council peered out from behind the High Table.

"Is that Prince Jacob?" said one of them.

Jacob walked round to the side of the upturned table.

"My Lords. Ladies. You must come with me at once. The royal guard have created a new perimeter ring around the outer palace walls for us to cast a barrier spell to protect whats left of the city."

They all looked at each other, some of them now standing up, but still remaining behind the High Table. Jacob looked at them outraged at their inaction.

"YOUR QUEEN IS IN THE FIGHT OF HER LIFE RIGHT NOW AND WE MUST SAVE THE CITY! I'M THE HIGHEST RANKING

MEMBER OF THIS COUNCIL. I COMMAND YOU!" Jacob
bellowed with such force it even frightened Elliot.

The council one by one got out from behind the table and
now followed Jacob out to the royal gardens atop the higher
palace that over looked the entire city. They could see the
ships from the American Republic of Magic still firing their
cannons into the outer city. Buildings crumbled one after the
other as they were struck. The fire was now spreading further
into the city towards the palace. Above them the Queen was
now summoning weather spells against Thomas. Ice, wind
and freezing rain was all sent hurtling towards him but he
blocked each element successfully whilst counter attacking
with his own lightening spells cracking into the Queen's
equally successful defence spells but Jacob could see they
were weakening. The barrier had to be summoned now if
only to protect his mother from Thomas' strengthening
attack. Jacob motioned the nine council members to the edge
of the royal garden to look down at the four hundred foot
drop to the courtyard. The Royal Guards that Jacob and Elliot
had sent were leading the hundreds of people from the city
through the main courtyard entrance. The tall circular outer
wall that surrounded the palace was now lined with
hundreds of royal guards each of them with their golden
wielding spears dug into the ground awaiting the barrier
spell to be cast.

Jacob looked back at the council, *"You see the guards
surrounding the outer wall? Their spears will conduct and
strengthen our barrier spell. We must cast it together! As one!
It's the only hope we have of creating a barrier strong enough to*

shield us from their attack…Elliot? We need you here!" Jacob called over to Elliot and he came running to his side.

"Form a circle. Reach out and hold each other!" said Jacob as the now eleven of them formed a tight circle holding each other firmly. They all closed their eyes and dug deep into the power and began to summons the barrier spell. Jacob struggled to concentrate as he could hear the constant cracking and booming from the spells his mother and Thomas were casting upon each other but he felt Elliot's hands in his which brought calmness to his mind. A swirling gust of wind began to engulf the group as sparks of bright light started to appear above them twisting and swirling as they began to join into one bright sphere of blinding light a few feet above them. The group felt the power vibrating through their bodies and into the sphere of light as it grew even brighter and then with a flash of intense light a straight beam of white light shot into the sky until it began to anvil a thousand feet above them forming perfect Dome edges falling towards the ground. The guards wielding spears began to glow a bright white and each of the hundreds of spears shot white beams of light meeting the edges still falling down from the barrier spell sealing the barrier dome shut.

The entire palace and its grounds were encased like a winter snow globe.

"We did it! It worked! It actually worked!" exclaimed Jacob with joy. Suddenly Elliot grabbed Jacob and forced his gaze to the sky toward his mother.

"JACOB! Your mother!" Elliot cried as the most powerful shockwave blew in the sky that even made the stones crack underneath their feet. Thomas had cast an enormous pushing spell in what looked like a last ditch attempt to overpower the Queen and it had worked. It was too powerful for her to block and struck her hard. Falling out of the sky towards the ground unconscious.

"MOTHER!" Jacob screamed as he leapt into the air with an air spell and flew towards his mother at such speed the sound broke around him.

Thomas saw Jacob flying towards his mother in an attempt to save her and summoned more bolts of lightening at them both. Jacob flew from side to side dodging the lightening as he caught his mother mid-air in his arms. He looked down at her unable to tell if she was alive or not.

"Mother wake up! PLEASE!" pleaded Jacob as lightening shot down each side of him but she did not respond.

Her eyes closed, her body lifeless in his arms. Jacob looked up at Thomas who was still floating a hundred feet above him, still inside the new barrier now protecting the palace. As Jacob looked at him floating there he felt a rage he'd never felt before. It grew stronger and stronger as he stared at him, his body on fire with hate and a power so strong the air around them began to spark alight with blue fire. As Jacob held his mother he felt this new power around him, it was dangerous, pure and raw but he felt in control of it. He focused his mind on the blue flames swirling around him and sent them like burning arrows straight at Thomas as he summoned a barrier defence spell, but as the flames hit his defence barrier it instantly began to weaken, forcing Thomas to fly backwards under the pressure of Jacob's powerful spell. As Thomas was weakened further he was finally pushed outside of the city barrier spell with Jacob's blue flames now spreading along the domed wall of the barrier. Thomas realising he was no longer inside the barrier tried to summons spell after spell striking the palace's barrier but it was too strong. The joint summoning effort of the Royal Council and the royal guards barrier spell to protect the palace had worked. Even the cannon fire from the American ships had no affect on the barrier.

Jacob was still floating just above the palace holding his mother in his arms. He looked down at the courtyard and saw the masters and MagiWolfs that were behind the palace walls had been defeated by the royal guards and most of the city's MagiFolk were safely behind the palace barrier. Thomas and his allies couldn't penetrate through the barrier either. They had saved the people and the palace from destruction.
He looked at his mother who was still lifeless and unresponsive, tears filling in his eyes.

"We did it mum. I did what you said. Now wake up...please!" Jacob sobbed as he began to float down back to the royal gardens. Elliot and the Royal Council gathered around watching as he landed softly resting The Queen, his mother carefully upon the grass covered ground. He knelt over her, tears falling fast, his hands shaking. He looked up at Elliot who knelt beside him with his arm holding Jacob.

"My hands...their shaking too much...I...I...can't feel her pulse, Elliot. She can't be, can she? Tell me she's not..." Elliot hugged him close and then reached down to the Queen's neck feeling for her pulse. All of the Royal Council looked on, their hands over their mouths and tears falling as they pleaded for a sign of life from the Queen.

"It's faint...but yes! There's a pulse! Jacob! She's still with us!" Said Elliot as Jacob hugged him in delight. *"Oh thank the kings!"* Cried out Jacob as the others fell to the ground in relief.

"She needs help though. Now! Someone fetch us a doctor from the palace infirmary" ordered Elliot as two of the guards ran from the gardens to find a doctor. *"She'll be okay, Jacob. She just needs rest. She's the strongest person I've ever known. A spell like that should have killed her instantly"* continued Elliot.

"I thought that was it, Elliot. I thought I'd lost her" said Jacob the tears still streaming down is face.

"I know. We all did" Said Elliot

"All I could think about is how I didn't take her hand last night on the ship. How she must have felt. How I...made her feel" Jacob sank his head into his mother's chest. Elliot rested his hand on Jacob's back comfortingly.

"She understood, Jacob. She always understands us. Even when we don't. I guess it's part of being a mother and a Queen. The question is...what do we do now" Elliot and Jacob looked

out over the city. Beyond the barrier the outer city was still burning fiercely and the ships of the American Republic of Magic were laying siege to everything on their side of the barrier.

"*They took the city,*" said Elliot sternly.

"*But they didn't take the Empire,*" replied Jacob his tears drying and his expression solemn as the doctor arrived with two nurses carrying a stretcher to help the Queen. Jacob and Elliot gently lifted her onto the stretcher.

"*We will take the Queen to her apartment in the higher palace and set up a private infirmary for her there, your highness,*" said the doctor. Jacob smiled and nodded softly in reply as they carried her away.

Jacob and Elliot could see the the nine Royal Council members talking amongst themselves as they looked over at Jacob.

"*This isn't over, Jacob. They need leadership, for that matter the entire country does,*" said Elliot. Jacob motioned his head towards the council indicating Elliot to accompany him as he walked over to them. As the two walked up to the council all talking stopped and all focused on Jacob.

"*I would suggest we go to the council chamber and discuss the situation we find ourselves in but as the chamber is blown to pieces…this…*" Jacob pointed to the gardens surrounding them "*will have to do!*" a few laughs and chuckles murmured as Royal Lady Black stepped forward. A short, slight and dark haired woman in her late fifties with dirt and blood stains across her face.

"Your highness. In light of your mother, the Queen being indisposed and your father the prince assumed captured at the White Islands this quorum of the Royal Council recognises you as the temporary reigning regent of the British Empire of Magic...or at least what's left of it. Do you accept?" said Lady Black as she pointed out to the burning outer city.

Jacob looked at Elliot and took his hand in his as he remembered his mother's words of advice to him onboard the Sabre.

Jacob nodded in submission *"I do accept. On one condition"* the council looked at Jacob eager to hear what the condition was. *"Elliot here, is to be made Royal Lord and co-regent until my mother regains her strength enough to resume her reign."* Elliot snapped his head round to look at Jacob, his eyebrows raised so high they crinkled the skin on his forehead into deep lines. Royal Lady Black stepped back in surprise of Jacobs request and looked back at her fellow council members who all equally had looks of surprise across their faces.

"Your highness, there hasn't been a co-regency for centuries!" exclaimed Lady Black.

"My mother expressed her wishes to me very clearly last night. If...and when I become her successor, she suggested Elliot should be at my side...and Lady Black? Take a look around you.

These are indeed unprecedented times which call for unprecedented changes. Don't you think?"

The Royal Lady turned her head around to assess the rest of the councils feelings as they all nodded in agreement to Jacob's conditions she smiled begrudgingly at Jacob and nodded to Elliot.

"Very well. The Royal Council officially recognises your temporary co-regency. King Jacob and co-regent Royal Lord Elliot" the council all bowed their heads in respect of their new King. Elliot keeping his head straight darted his wide open eyes over at Jacob who was concentrating very hard not to burst out laughing at Elliot's expression.

"I hope you have a plan, your majesty. A mere quarter of our forces remain and our entire navy sank" said Royal Lady Black plainly.

"I do...or shall I say the Queen does. Our hopes rest with Royal Lady Kerr and convincing the French to help us. For now, we are safe behind the barrier, but Thomas is more powerful and cunning than we ever thought possible...in time he will find a way through. We just need to make sure we are ready. I will reach out to Parliament in the meantime, they will need our help. While Thomas was unsuccessful in the destruction of the Royal Council I believe his focus will change to seeking out and controlling the members of Parliament themselves" Said Jacob.

"I sent word to Parliament as soon as the attack started here your majesty. Procedure for this situation, in the event the Palace is taken by an enemy force is for Parliament House and

its members to seal themselves within their chambers at Dover Cliff" Said Lady Black.

"Good, Dover Cliff is as secure as the Palace, if not more so. For now if you'll excuse me counsellors, I would like to go to my mothers side... Elliot? Join me, please."

Elliot still in a daze over the events that had just passed shook his head and walked with Jacob back into the higher palace halls. Once out of ear shot from the council Elliot pulled on Jacob's robes sleeve.

"What just happened?" Elliot asked his eyes wide like a puppy.

Jacobs laughed but continued walking "Well. You're a Royal Lord. Actually you're a Royal Lord and a co-regent, if that's even a thing...I suppose it is now!"

"Why did you do that? I never asked for..." but Jacob stopped still and cupped Elliots face in his hands.

"You didn't ask for this, I know...and neither did I...But I can't do this without you. My mother was right, I need you with me by my side. We are at war and we are losing, plus I have no idea what I'm doing".

"Oh! And you think I do!?" Said Elliot as his laughs echoed down the sandy coloured stone hall.

"I think between the two of us and Camila?...we might just be able to figure it out. At least until mother is strong enough"

Elliot looked down the hall at the door leading to the Queen's apartment with nurses rushing in and out.

"I guess we're doing this!" said Elliot

"I guess we are!" said Jacob.

TO BE CONTINUED...

ABOUT THE AUTHOR

Joseph J. Jordan is the author of 'The British Empire of Magic' the first novella of a trilogy. Starting his writing career in December 2020 during the UK COVID-19 lockdown and finishing his first novella 'The British Empire of Magic' in February 2021. Enjoy his work now on Amazon Kindle.

If you enjoyed this novella please leave a kind review on The British Empire of Magic Amazon product page.

ACKNOWLEDGEMENTS

My writing journey would not have been possible without the support and encouragement of my mother.

Thank you to Joanna Jordan for her editing contribution throughout. I could not have shared this story without you.

Printed in Great Britain
by Amazon